Tommy Ellis Heads North West

Jes Parkin

Tommy Ellis Heads North West

Published by

Stella Books

ISBN: 978-0-9929325-2-7

Also by Jes Parkin

TOMMY ELLIS GOES TO SEA

In memory of all the fishermen

who sailed from our shores,

never to return.

Acknowledgements

My thanks to Ray Hawker, retired trawler skipper, for sharing his knowledge of the deep sea fishing grounds around Greenland, and for kindly donating books to use in my research.

To the Hull Bullnose Heritage Group for their continuous support.

To Peter O'Connor of BespokeBookCovers.com for the cover design.

To Claire Wingfield, editor, for her invaluable advice and guidance.

To Ron Harrison of 'Total Web Fusion', for solving my IT problems as well as designing a wonderful website for me.

To Sherry Pilisko, an Angel in disguise.

To my family and friends for their love and support.

'I must go down to the seas again, for the call of the running tide, Is a wild call, and a clear call that may not be denied'

It is the summer of 1960. Tommy Ellis is on his second trip to sea on the trawler, *Stella Vega*. What adventures lie in store for him this time?

CHAPTER ONE

"Where are we going this time, Dad?" asked Tommy from the back seat of the taxi. It was late on a balmy night at the end of July, and they were sailing on the midnight tide.

"Greenland, son. Didn't you know? That's why we both went to see Dr. MacBurns on the Fish Dock today for a medical. Everybody who goes to Greenland has to have a medical."

"Why? We didn't have a medical last year when we went to Bear Island," Tommy replied.

"Well, there are a couple of reasons. One is that Greenland is a very remote area and there's little chance of medical assistance if you need it. Another reason is the Inuit, the local people of Greenland. If one of them was exposed to the flu, or even a common cold, it could kill them."

Tommy was astonished. He had never heard of anyone dying of a cold before.

He thought back to his visit to Dr. MacBurns, a Scottish gentleman. The medical hadn't taken very long at all. The doctor had listened to his chest, checked his blood pressure, his height, his weight and his eyesight. Oddly, thought Tommy, he had made him do some squats before giving him the 'all clear'.

"We should get some good halibut around Greenland at this time of year, and the biggest cod you have ever seen. But don't tell a soul until after we've sailed," his father whispered, "we don't want every trawler from Hull following us."

Greenland was near Canada. Tommy had studied Canada in his geography lessons at school and was fascinated by the hundreds of small islands in the Polar regions to the north of the country. He had read a book called 'The Northwest Passage', about a voyage of exploration by a Norwegian explorer, Roald Amundsen, and another about John Franklin, the British explorer who never returned from his journey to the North West in the 1800's.

Tommy thought of his trip to Bear Island with his father the previous summer. It had been much colder than he expected and he needed to wear a thick woollen guernsey to keep him warm all the time they were beyond the Arctic Circle. But the bitter cold Amundsen described was nothing Tommy had ever experienced before. How would he survive?

On the approach to the tunnel in West Dock Avenue, leading to the fish dock, his father broke the silence that hung between them, "The Mate's son, Robert is coming with us this time. You'll be able to show him the ropes."

"Oh good." Tommy was surprised. He hadn't thought another boy would be joining them on the trip. "Is it the same Mate as last year?" he asked.

"Yes, Jacko. Bill Jackson. You remember him don't you?"

Tommy thought back to the man who allowed him to go in the ambulance with him to take Mike to the hospital in Norway, and how kind he had been. He frowned as he also remembered going overboard in bad weather, but only because he had saved the Mate from a nasty accident. The recollection of being in the freezing cold Arctic sea sent an icy cold shiver right down his spine and he shuddered at the thought. He'd had a dream about drowning the night before sailing on the last trip, but not this time. This time, all that had kept him awake was the thrill of going back to sea.

Coming out of the tunnel at the far end, Tommy saw all around familiar hustle and bustle of cars, lorries, trucks and people. The same clip-clop-clatter sounds of the clogs worn by many of the dock workers, the same queue of taxis, and the same groups of fishermen waiting with their kit bags, ready to go on board. Both Tommy and his father turned their heads in the direction of a sudden raucous laughter they heard not far from the taxi. There was a small group of fishermen laughing loudly and staggering from side to side.

"If they were my crew I wouldn't let them on board."

Tommy knew many of the fishermen drank a lot, but it didn't cross his mind they would turn up for their ships drunk.

"What happens if their skipper doesn't let them on board, Dad?"

"They'll be sent back home and it'll be a while before they get another trip. No trip means no money. They'd think twice about turning up drunk again. There are always plenty of men over by the lock hoping to catch a trip if someone doesn't turn up."

As he finished speaking they pulled over and joined the queue of taxis. Tommy recognised Bert Cooper, the Company Runner, wearing the same sheepskin jacket, the same flat cap and holding what could have been the same clip-board and pencil in his hands. Bert was approached by another person. Tommy thought his eyes were playing tricks on him. He squinted and looked again. He was amazed to recognise Mike Beech, the Deckie Learner from his previous trip. He was talking with Bert. Tommy could see he was wearing a dark jacket, and noticed the right sleeve was pinned up to the shoulder. Memories of Mike's accident came flooding back to him again; how his arm was cut to the bone by the cable that gave way on the deck; sailing at full speed to reach Hammerfest on the North Cape of Norway so Mike could receive hospital treatment; learning Mike's arm couldn't be saved, and then leaving him behind, all alone, in the hospital in Norway.

"Dad, look. There's Mike."

"So there is, son," his father replied, following the direction Tommy was pointing. "Why don't you go and say hello to him? I'm sure he'll be pleased to see you. I'm going straight on board after I've spoken to Bert. You can join us in a few minutes. The *Stella Vega* is about half way down the dock side." He waved towards a row of trawlers on the far side of the dock.

Tommy was out of the taxi like a shot. "Mike! Mike!" he shouted.

"Well I never." exclaimed Mike, looking Tommy up and down, with the same cheeky grin, the same sparkling eyes and the same quiff flopping down over his forehead. "Don't tell me you're going on another trip? You are a glutton for punishment, aren't you?"

"Yeah. Here we go again! But tell me, how are you? Are you working for the Company now?"

Mike smiled. "That's right. I'm learning how to be a Company Runner. Come on, I'll walk you to the ship and tell you all about it on the way. If we stay here gassing all night you'll miss the tide."

As they crossed over the lock gates to the other side of the dock, Mike told Tommy of his despair when he found out he had lost his arm, knowing he wouldn't be able to go to sea again, and feeling very sorry for himself. His journey from Hammerfest to Bergen wasn't too bad as they put him on a ferry instead of a train. He was glad of that as he didn't like trains very much. The ra-ta-ta-ta rattling sound they made over the rails got on his nerves. When he got to Bergen the boat for Newcastle was there, ready to sail, and the next morning he was back in England. His parents made the journey to Newcastle to meet him off the ship and boy, was Mike glad to see them. He had expected to see his mother cry, but it was the first time he had seen his father shed tears. The three of them hugged tightly before making their way to the station to catch the train to Hull. Back in

Hull, Mike had to report to a specialist, Mr Dickinson, at the Hull Royal Infirmary, who would be taking care of him. He was told, as soon as he was fit enough, he had to report to the Company offices on St. Andrews Dock. The rest was history, so to speak.

"Well, here you are Tommy Ellis, delivered safe and sound to the *Stella Vega*," Mike said cheerfully. "I wish I was going with you," he murmured quietly as he cast his eyes over the vessel.

"So do I." Tommy felt Mike's sadness.

Mike extended his left hand to shake Tommy's. "Have a good trip. See you when you get back." He smiled.

Tommy didn't hesitate to reach out and take Mike's hand.

"Yes. We'll have to keep in touch."

Mike smiled again, "That'll be nice." But before turning to walk away he added, "Oh, by the way, I hear you've got the Mate's lad on board, young Robert. Watch out for that one. He's always in trouble."

Tommy thought, "Great. That's all I need." Then he watched as Mike smiled, turned and sauntered away. He really did wish Mike was going with them.

CHAPTER TWO

Tommy stepped on board with the swagger of a confident, experienced fisherman. His head was held high and he was feeling optimistic about the trip ahead. Going through the doorway, the familiar sounds and smells came back to him, the pulsating sound of the engine that made the floor and walls vibrate, and the smell of oil and grease. He could also smell fresh paint. He made sure he walked in the centre of the passageway as he didn't want to get wet paint on his clothes. He remembered his way round the *Stella Vega* and when he reached his cabin he found that his kit bag and mattress had been thrown onto his bunk. The same bunk in the same cabin as last trip. After unpacking and putting his things away, he went to the galley to find Tom Fletcher. He poked his head around the door and, sure enough, old Tom was there. The same wrinkly, crusty looking fellow, sleeves rolled up to his elbows and forearms full of scars.

"Evening, Cook. Any jobs need doing?"

The Cook turned his head, his eyes creased up as he looked at Tommy and declared, "Well would you believe it? Look who we have here. Come back for more punishment, have you? Nothing to do down here at the moment, so you can take some tea up to your dad if you like."

"Alright Cook, I'll do that," Tommy replied, thinking

that Cook was still as grumpy as ever.

"Come back in the morning and bring the Mate's lad with you. You can both help Brian peel the tayties."

"Is Brian here?" Tommy asked while helping himself to the tea, sugar, milk and teapot, remembering where everything was kept.

"He's putting the stores away. You'll see him soon enough," Cook replied.

"Nice to see you again," Tommy laughed as he left the galley. He made his way up to the bridge where he found his father and Norman, the Radio Operator. Norman invited Tommy to join him in the Radio Room any time he felt like it, then Tommy's father, the Skipper, noticed Jacko, the Mate and his son pull up alongside in a taxi.

"Here they are at last. Tommy, go down and meet them and show Robert to your cabin. He'll be sharing with you. The Deckie Learner has gone in with the spare hands."

Until that moment, Tommy hadn't thought who the Deckie Learner might be. But he knew he would meet him soon enough.

"Hiya Tommy." The Mate's face lit up as Tommy approached. "Good to see you again. This is Robert. I'm sure you two will get on just fine."

Robert was a bit younger than Tommy, maybe ten or eleven. He was wearing a black woolly balaclava type hat;

a black bomber jacket, zipped up to the top and round his neck he was wearing a black and amber striped scarf. Black and amber were the colours of their local football team, Hull City. He had both hands in his pockets and his shoulders were hunched forward as he looked down to the wellington boots he was wearing on his feet. Tommy was amused to see him wearing his cold weather clothes before they had even set sail.

"Say hello to Tommy, Robert. He'll be looking after you during the trip." The Mate nudged his son forward.

Robert lifted his head slightly and Tommy saw he was pulling the biggest pet lip he had ever seen. He thought, "If he pulls that lip out any further, he'll trip up over it."

"Come on, Robert. I'll show you to our cabin." Sensing Robert was feeling anxious, Tommy said, as they were walking along the passageways, "It's not that bad, you know. We'll be helping the Cook in the galley most of the time, but we'll have other jobs to do as well."

Robert didn't answer as he followed Tommy to their cabin. Tommy even helped him carry his kit bag and mattress, but Robert was silent. When they reached the cabin, Tommy put Robert's things on his bunk.

"You'll be sleeping here. I'm in that bunk over there."He pointed to the far side of the small triangular room. Robert took off his balaclava, but not his scarf, and used his fingers in an attempt to tidy his dark brown hair which had a very neat and very straight parting from the crown of his head to just above his left eyebrow. His eyes looked shifty as they darted from left to right. Looking round the room, he wrinkled his nose in disgust.

"I'm not sleeping in here. It stinks."

Tommy was taken aback.

"You'll get used to it, and we never close the door so we can get plenty of fresh air inside." He tried to sound convincing. "Anyway, we should be sailing soon. Let's go on the bridge and watch as we go through the lock." He continued wanting to sound encouraging and reassuring, although he was thinking it might be hard to get along with this miserable looking kid.

Robert didn't reply, but with his hands in his pockets he followed Tommy along the passageway and up the stairs. While they were making their way to the bridge, Tommy tried to start a friendly conversation with Robert, saying,

"You're a Hull City supporter, are you? Do you go to Boothferry Park to watch them play?"

"Yeah." was the sullen reply.

"Who do you go with?" Tommy kept trying.

"Grandad." Another one word answer.

Tommy was relieved when they soon arrived at the wheelhouse. His father, the Skipper and Robert's father, the Mate were both talking to Norman, the Radio Operator. The Skipper saw the two boys and said,

"Ah, here you are, just in time, we're about to cast off. Stand over there by the window the pair of you. Looking forward to your trip, Robert?"

"Suppose so."

"Robert," said the Mate, frowning. "Stand up straight and mind your manners. There are lots of young lads in Hull wishing they were in your shoes right now."

Tommy wasn't looking forward to the next three weeks pandering to Robert's moods. Mike had said he was always in trouble and Tommy wondered what sort of trouble.

"Away forward! Away aft!" The Skipper shouted his orders and they were on their way.

As they left St Andrews Dock and sailed through the lock, out into the River Humber, Tommy started to feel the movement of the *Stella Vega* beneath his feet. He breathed deeply through his nose, filling his lungs with the smell of the sea. Already he detected a change in the air and anticipated the fresh tang of the salty spray which lay ahead of them once they were out of the river and heading north in the North Sea.

It was gone midnight and it was dark outside. As they sailed out of the lock and into the River Humber, all that could be seen on the shore were the twinkling lights of a city at sleep. Tommy tried hard, but couldn't make out the sights of Hull in the dark. Looking forward to his jobs the next day, he decided it was time to go to bed. He showed

Robert where the washrooms and toilets were before telling him a few things about his first trip and how he was looking forward to doing it all again. He missed out the bit about going overboard and Mike's accident.

"I didn't want to come, but my dad made me."

"Why did he make you?"

Robert glared back at Tommy.

"That's really none of your business."

CHAPTER THREE

Tommy woke up the next morning, the first full day of the trip, and saw Robert's bunk was empty. He checked his watch and seeing that it was only a quarter past six, he thought Robert might already be in the galley helping cook with the breakfasts. Thinking of breakfast Tommy's mouth started watering as the smell of freshly baked bread wafted through the passageways and into his cabin. When he got out of his bunk and put his feet on the floor, he felt the familiar rolling of the ship as well as the vibration and throbbing of the engines as they pulsated deep below the deck. It was like coming home. This was where he belonged, on the high seas. He quickly washed his face, brushed his teeth and hurried to the galley.

Tommy was glad to see Brian, the Galley Boy, again. He recognised him straightaway; same freckles, same smile with the same crooked front teeth, and was that a bit of stubble sticking out around his chin? He was even wearing what looked to be the same grubby apron. Brian's shoulders were a bit broader though, and maybe he had grown an inch or so in height. But he was still quite short for a seventeen year old.

"Hiya Brian," he said, on entering the galley. "No more hamsters this trip I hope?"

Brian laughed. "No way. I gave it to my seven-year-old cousin, Peter. Aunty Jean doesn't mind them, not like my mum. Anyway, they still call him Cookie."

Tommy giggled and Brian let out a throaty chuckle.

The Cook, who was busy frying bacon and eggs, turned to the boys and said,

"Haven't you two got anything better to do than stand around gossiping like old washerwomen?"

The boys laughed and chattered cheerfully as they got on with their chores of preparing the tables in the mess and making sure there was plenty of hot tea in the pot, ready for the crew when they came in from the deck.

Robert should have been helping in the galley, but he was nowhere to be seen. Perhaps he was with his father, who would be out on the deck at this time of the morning.

There was an hour or so to spare before helping Brian peel the tayties, so Tommy went up to the bridge. His heart swelled as he walked the familiar passageways and climbed the stairs. He took a deep breath as he stepped through the door leading to the wheelhouse.

"Hiya Tommy," his father greeted him before turning to check the charts.

Tommy stepped into the Radio Room where he saw Norman was busy tapping out messages.

"Come on in, lad. You can help me with these messages."

Tommy didn't understand morse code but asked what he could do.

"Crew like to send telegrams to the people at home to wish them a Happy Birthday, Happy Anniversary or Merry Christmas when they are away for Christmas. Look," he continued, picking up a pile of hand-written messages, "read these out to me one at a time. I know it's a bit soon for some of the messages, but I'm sending them through to Wick Radio and they will hang on to them and send the telegrams on the right date."

Tommy found a stool and perched next to the Radio Operator, and read from the pieces of paper, one by one. Some of the messages were in a code he didn't understand, but Norman explained that SWALK meant 'Sealed With A Loving Kiss' and HOLLAND meant 'Hope Our Love Lasts And Never Dies'. Tommy blushed as he wasn't used to all this lovey-dovey stuff.

The Skipper poked his head around the door.

"Want to take the wheel?" he asked, eyes twinkling.

Tommy grinned and returned to the bridge. He checked the course and the compass, took the wheel in both hands and looked forward, pointing the ship towards the far horizon. It was a bright morning and a gleaming early morning sun shone over the sea, making it look like a wavy carpet, filled with millions and millions of sparkling diamonds. It was so bright he had to squint his eyes to see properly. There was a slight swell, but no big waves, allowing the *Stella Vega* to travel at full speed ahead.

"Where are we now, Dad?" Tommy asked his father, who was in the chart room just behind the bridge, talking to the Radio Operator.

"A few miles east of Aberdeen. If you look carefully, you might be able to see the coast on the port side." He came to stand by Tommy's side.

Tommy looked to port and he could just make out the faint, dark line of the coast on the horizon.

The Radio Operator stuck his head through the bridge doorway.

"You wanted a forecast for the Pentland Firth, Skipper?"

Tommy's father stepped into the Radio Room.

"What's the Pentland Firth?" asked Tommy.

His father returned to the bridge to stand by him. "It's the stretch of water that lies between the north coast of Scotland and the Orkney Islands. It can be dangerous sometimes because there are seven different tides coming from different directions. One minute the sea is flat calm and the next there are waves crashing over the deck. And when you get one tide coming from one direction meeting another from a different direction, they can easily form a whirlpool."

Tommy had read adventure stories and seen films of pirates at sea, and of when they came across whirlpools, looking like water swirling down a giant plug-hole in a giant sink, and how ships were sucked into them, dragged down by the whirling movement, gyrating round and round.

"The only other way to the Atlantic is to keep going north and sail around the islands. The trawler owners don't like us to sail through the Pentland Firth, but if we do, it can save us a full day. It's just the short stretch of water between Duncansby Head, on the North Eastern point of Scotland, and Dunnet Head, just a bit further along the coast. So, if it gets a bit rough, hold tight!"

Tommy stayed at the wheel for a while longer, once again imagining being the captain of a ship himself one day, sailing across all the oceans of the world, dodging whirlpools and tacking into and around gigantic waves. He liked the sound of 'Captain Tommy Ellis'. During the past year he had read a lot of books about the sea. As well as the tales of the search for the Northwest Passage, he read books by an author called C. S. Forester, who wrote stories about a man called Horatio Hornblower. Hornblower started going to sea as a young boy and the stories followed his career in the Royal Navy. He started as Midshipman; progressed to Captain, fighting the French in the Napoleonic Wars and eventually became Admiral of the Fleet. In those days the ships were wooden galleons with big sails, and canons on and below the deck for battle.

Tommy stared down at the sparkling sea for just a few minutes more and then shook himself out of his daydream, thinking it must be time to go and help Brian peel the tayties.

One of the deck hands came up to take over the wheel from him and he bounced back down the stairs to look for Brian.

CHAPTER FOUR

Cook was in a terrible mood. Tommy found him in the galley muttering and mumbling to himself about Robert being trouble, and he was banging pans and other utensils around on the worktops.

Tommy was almost afraid to interrupt, so he coughed quietly hoping the Cook wouldn't turn on him. Cook turned with a sharp movement, and glared as he saw Tommy.

"Cook?" Tommy shrank in the doorway.

"It's alright lad," Cook whispered. "If you're looking for Brian he's made a start on the tayties. I think he's aft, on the boat deck." Then, changing the tone of his voice, he barked, "But don't expect to find young Robert there. Peeling tayties is beneath him, apparently. Shouldn't have been allowed on board if you ask me."

"Alright Cook. See ya." Tommy took his leave as quietly as he came, and made his way to the boat deck to help Brian. Robert had obviously upset Cook. Tommy wondered if he was going to be badly behaved for the rest of the trip. He hoped not. He hoped that he would settle down soon and accept that life on a trawler was hard, but could be enjoyable too.

Early that afternoon, when all the pots had been washed

and put away, Tommy went back to the bridge to see his father, who said,

"Go and find Robert. The two of you can help Deckie with the greasing."

Tommy remembered having to go down into the engine room on his last trip to ask for bollard grease, the thick, gooey stuff he had to rub onto some of the surfaces of the ship.

"Who's the Deckie Learner this time?" He asked his father, sad that Mike wasn't with them on this trip.

"Danny Draper. Been with us a couple of trips and was hoping to sign on as Spare Hand this time. The Company promised him one more trip as Deckie Learner, then they'll give him the job. He's a good lad, hard-working, and I think he's ready for the step up the ladder."

It often happened that some of the crew already had their Mate's tickets or even their Skipper's tickets and Tommy wondered why they were still working as deck hands. Maybe they had to wait for a vacancy?

Everybody on the bridge turned round as they heard a loud rumpus coming towards them. The Bosun, Harry Hunter, was dragging a loudly protesting Robert through the bridge door by the scruff of his neck while shouting,

"Do you know where I found this little beggar? Do you know? He was half way up the radar scanner. Half way up the scanner, he was." Tommy noticed his teeth were rattling and moving around in his mouth and bits of spit were spraying out as he spoke.

All the time he was speaking, Robert was thrashing his arms about, yelling, "Get off me. Get off me. You're hurting me."

"I will hurt you if I catch you up there again." The Bosun spat the words out before turning to the Skipper. "I was on the deck and something caught the corner of my eye. When I looked up there he was, hanging onto the scanner with one hand and his City scarf flapping behind him in the wind."

Harry Hunter, the Bosun, was a big hefty man with a barrel-shaped chest. He wore a greasy looking flat cap and a red cotton neckerchief tied loosely around his neck. His dark blue guernsey fit snugly about him and was tucked into the tops of his trousers. His face was so red and blotchy with rage, it reminded Tommy of corned beef.

"Thanks Harry, I'll deal with this now." The Skipper's voice was stern and clipped as he nodded his head to the Bosun.

Harry let go of Robert and turned away, shaking his head and mumbling to himself, "Whatever next? That lad's going to be trouble. You can bet your life he's going to be trouble."

That was exactly what Mike and Cook had said.

The Skipper frowned at Robert and asked, "What were you doing up the scanner?"

"I only wanted a better view," came Robert's surly reply.

"A trawler is not a playground," said the Skipper sharply. "It is a place of work and a very dangerous place of work too. You do not climb up radar scanners or anything else while you're here. Do you understand?"

"I didn't do anything wrong, and you're not my dad," Robert shouted, glaring back at the Skipper. "You can't tell me what to do."

Tommy's eyes nearly popped out of his head.

"I can't tell you what to do?" The Skipper's voice boomed around the bridge. "If we were still in the River Humber, I'd have you put ashore immediately. I am the Skipper on board this trawler and everybody, and that includes you, does as I say. Do you understand?"

But Robert had the cheek to tut, roll his eyes, stick his hands back in his pockets and sway his shoulders from side to side, completely untouched by the telling off, showing no remorse at all.

At that moment, Robert's dad came storming onto the bridge, panting.

"The Bosun's just told me what happened. I'm sorry Skipper. It won't happen again." Then, turning to Robert he said in a gentle voice, as though to mollify him, "You won't do that again, will you son? You did promise you'd be a good lad didn't you? Now say you're sorry to the Skipper." The Mate then turned to Tommy and said,

"Will you keep an eye on him Tommy? You've been here before and you know the ropes."

"Whoa, steady on there, Jacko." The Skipper interjected. "My lad is not going to be held responsible for your lad in any way, shape or form. No way. He can help Tommy with his chores and Tommy will show him how things are done, but if he wanders off and gets into mischief, that's his own fault. Is that clear?"

"Yes, Skipper." The Mate placed one hand on Roberts shoulder as though to protect him and looked down at the floor.

"Take him down to the galley. I'm sure Cook will have a few jobs to keep him busy and out of trouble."

The Mate and his son left the bridge, the Mate mumbling several more times, "Sorry Skipper."

After they left, Tommy spoke first, but he didn't tell his father there had already been problems between Robert and the Cook.

"Mike told me Robert was in trouble."

"Yes, son," his father replied steadily. "We had all better watch out for that one."

"What sort of trouble has he been in?" Tommy asked. "On land, I mean."

The Skipper pondered for a few seconds as he looked at Tommy before saying,

"This has to stay between you and me, so you won't tell anyone else, will you?"

"No, Dad. Promise." Tommy replied crossing his heart with his right index finger.

"They've had the police round at the house a few times. He's been breaking into neighbours' sheds. Not to steal anything, just to make a mess, like tipping paint all over the place and emptying boxes of nails all over the floor. He was expelled from school just after the half term because he deliberately smashed some laboratory equipment and when the teacher apprehended him, he kicked her in the legs. The last straw was when he got hold of the neighbour's cat, tied it to a fence and turned the hosepipe on it. People as far away as the next street heard the poor thing screaming. Others in the family thought a trip to sea might do him good, that it might make a good lad out of him."

"Do you think it will, Dad?"

CHAPTER FIVE

Tommy went down to the deck to help Danny Draper, the Deckie Learner. Although he'd never met him, he spotted him straight away with his tin of bollard grease and a piece of rag in his hand, but Tommy was surprised. Danny looked much older than Mike or Brian, who were still youths. Danny had the build of a man, not a boy, although he was only eighteen years of age. Danny was about five feet ten inches tall. He had dark hair sticking out from under a dirty looking cloth cap, and long sideburns curling down his cheeks in front of his ears. His broad shoulders were prominent under a dark guernsey that was tucked into a pair of grey fearnought trousers, which were fastened round the waist with a broad leather belt. His rubber sea boots had been turned down to below the knees. Danny smiled as Tommy approached.

"I was hoping you'd come and give me a hand," he said cheerfully in a deep, yet soft sounding voice. "I'm Danny, the Deckie Learner. But not for much longer, I hope. They said one more trip, then I can move up to Deck Hand," he continued, and his eyes were gazing somewhere far off in the distance.

Tommy gathered Danny was ambitious and thought, that one day soon, he might be in Danny's shoes, at the start of a life at sea. But would that be on a trawler as a Deckie

Learner? He was expected to stay on at school and take his 'O' Level G.C.E. examinations. He would be sixteen then. Would it be too late? Would he be too old? Lots of Deckie Learners started at the age of fifteen after a couple of trips as Galley Boy. If he didn't go on the trawlers, he could always go to the Nautical College to study to be an officer in the Merchant Navy and sail on big boats. He had heard that five trips on a trawler would get you a place in the Nautical College anyway, and wondered if his father would agree to him getting in that way. The Nautical College had a nice new building down George Street in the town centre, and all the students wore a smart naval uniform, similar to that worn by the boys at the Trinity House School.

Thoughts of what he might do in the future drifted through Tommy's mind while he was greasing the scuppers on the port side of the ship. He could feel the sea breeze whip across his face as he worked, and he could taste the salt on his lips. His legs were steady on the deck as the *Stella Vega* rolled easily over the gentle swell of the sea. The sun had moved further over to the west, but was now surrounded by fluffy, white candy floss clouds hanging heavy with dark grey weighing down their bellies. He hoped it wouldn't rain.

He listened to the banter of the deck hands as they worked. Some of their jokes he didn't understand, but their peals of laughter told him they must have been very funny. Someone shouted out,

"Where's our music?"

The Skipper leaned out of the bridge window, giving the

thumbs up sign. Within a couple of minutes, Country and Western music was blaring out over the loud speakers and the men sang along with the familiar tunes, cowboy songs. The fishermen liked cowboy songs and often spoke about the latest cowboy film they had seen whilst they were ashore. Sometimes they discussed which was the best cowboy film ever, and who the best cowboy was.

Tommy couldn't help but notice an old man he had never seen before. He was sitting up on the foredeck, all alone, mending nets. He looked much older than anyone else on board, even older than Cook. His broad, heavy shoulders were rounded as he bent forward to work. He wasn't wearing a cap and his white hair was short and sticking up straight as though he'd had an electric shock. Danny came over to where Tommy was working and saw him looking at the man.

"That's Jeremiah Hobbs," he said, "and he expects everybody, even the Skipper, to call him Mr Hobbs."

"I haven't seen him before," Tommy said.

"No, he keeps himself to himself. Only does the Greenland trips. People say he's a bit crazy. They say he's looking for his brother who went down off Cape Farewell in the winter of 1952."

Tommy shivered. "That's sad. Does he think he's going to find him?"

"I don't know. I haven't sailed with him before. I've only heard the rumours."

During a brief pause between the songs, Tommy and Danny looked at each other as they heard a muffled,

"Help! Help!" and again "Help!"

Danny yelled up to the bridge and signalled the Skipper to stop the music, shouting, "Somebody's calling for help."

Everybody on deck downed tools and listened. Sure enough, the faint voice was heard again.

"Help! Help!" and every man on deck started checking here, there and everywhere to see where the voice was coming from. Some men went inside the forecastle to have a look, but soon came out shaking their heads. Nobody there. Some looked under the piles of nets on the deck, but again nothing. Two men went down into the fish room in the hold and it wasn't long before they shouted,

"Found him."

Everybody huddled round the top of the hatch, including the Skipper who had come down from the bridge to see who it was.

Tommy thought how, if someone was badly hurt, they would have to sail to the nearest port. He heard a whimper, "Get me out! Get me out!" and immediately recognised Robert's voice.

"Is he hurt?" the Skipper shouted to the men in the hold.

"Only his pride."

"Bring him up to the bridge. Jacko, come with me," he snarled at the Mate as he stormed off the deck.

A pathetic-looking Robert was lifted out of the hold, his Hull City scarf wrapped around his mouth and over his ears, and he didn't like it that everyone was laughing at him. But he did look a sorry sight. He was wet through, bedraggled and trembling with cold. Apparently, he'd decided to explore below deck and clambered up some wooden planks that were holding the ice, stored ready to be put on the fish when it was caught. He had lost his footing, fallen in and couldn't get out again.

"Shut up you lot. Stop laughing at me. I hate you. I hate all of you!" he screamed, which made the men laugh even more. Robert rubbed the back of his hand over his face as though to dry his tears as he ran from the deck.

Tommy felt sorry for Robert. He was such an unhappy boy. Maybe he just needed a friend.

Up on the bridge, the Skipper gave Robert the dressing down of his life, but the boy looked defiantly at the Skipper as he spoke.

"He is quite sensitive, you know," said the Mate.

"*Sensitive?*" replied the Skipper. "He is nothing but a spoilt brat and it's about time you taught him some discipline, and if you don't, then I will!"

Tommy finished his greasing work on the deck shortly after the Robert incident and returned to his cabin to find the young lad on his bunk, still with his scarf around his neck, reading a comic as though nothing had happened.

"Are you alright?" he asked.

"What's it to do with you?" snapped Robert.

"I only want to be your friend."

"Well I don't need any friends so leave me alone." He withdrew his chin and mouth into his scarf.

Tommy left the cabin wondering when Robert would realise he was mistaken.

CHAPTER SIX

Tommy kept a close lookout for whirlpools and big waves coming in over the calm sea, but he saw none. He had studied the charts and was able to identify Duncansby Head then Dunnet Head on the north coast of Scotland. He gave a sigh of relief when they passed Dunnet Head, as he knew they would no longer be in danger of coming across whirlpools, which his father also called 'eddys'.

"Skipper. Skipper," someone was shouting as they came up the stairs and onto the bridge. It was Cook and he didn't look happy.

"Will you come and look at this, Skipper? Come and look at the mess in my store room. I've never seen anything like it in my life. Never."

"What do you mean, Cook?" Tommy's father queried.

"Somebody has ransacked my store cupboard. There's stuff everywhere." Cook was shaking with rage.

Tommy followed Cook and the Skipper to the store room. It was in a terrible mess. Potatoes, carrots, apples and onions were all over the floor, flour had been scattered over everything, tins and containers had been dragged off the shelves and thrown about. The whole room was a scene of destruction.

"Who would do this?" asked Cook bewildered. "And why? I don't get it. It's never happened before."

"Would you like me to clean it up, Cook?" Tommy asked feeling sorry for the old man.

"No." His father was abrupt. "I think the culprit should be made to clear this lot up, and I think I know who it is."

Robert was found and brought to the storeroom. At first he denied all knowledge of the devastation, but then the Skipper bent over and looked him straight in the face saying,

"I know why you're here and what you've been up to ashore. I don't like liars and nor does anybody else here on board. People's lives could be at risk through your stupidity. Do you understand, boy?"

"I only did it for a laugh. The Cook is always picking on me and I thought I'd teach him a lesson, the miserable old beggar."

"Don't you dare disrespect the Cook or anyone else while you are on my ship," Tommy's father bellowed. "You will clean this lot up, now!" he shouted.

"I can't do it on my own. Tommy will have to help me," he whined, snuggling his chin into his scarf.

"Fat chance of that," said Tommy. He turned on his heels and left as Cook was handing Robert a sweeping brush.

The stories of Robert's escapades soon spread around the *Stella Vega*. The Cook reluctantly tried to keep Robert busy in the galley and the mess with chores such as washing dishes, mashing the tea and setting the tables ready for meal times, but Robert was not co-operating. He tackled all his jobs half-heartedly and either Tommy or Brian had to check on him and, more often than not, do the job again. The three boys would sit together on the boat deck to peel the tayties, but it was Tommy and Brian who did the work. Robert just sat watching them, complaining. He liked to climb up the railings and perch on the top. Both Brian and Tommy told him not to, as he could easily slip and fall overboard, but Robert didn't listen. Each time he was told, he replied in a haughty manner that he wasn't stupid and that he knew how to hold on tight. He said it was just like being on some of the rides at Hull Fair. The Cook referred to him as 'daft lad' as he had done with Tommy during his first trip and with Brian beforehand. But Robert did not take the name calling lightly. He answered back to the Cook and called him names in return.

Tommy and Danny, the Deckie Learner, had tried to get Robert to help with the greasing on deck, but he would have none of it. He said it was a messy job and he didn't see why he should have to get his hands dirty. So Danny decided it was Robert's job to go back and forth to the engine room to get more bollard grease when they needed it. Between trips to get the grease, Robert kicked his heels around the deck annoying people while they worked. If someone put down a tool and turned to look away, Robert would move it and the man had to look for it. Now and then someone shouted at him as he climbed onto the railings or up the mast. He didn't seem to sense the danger. All in all, Robert was a nuisance.

The unusually calm waters came to an abrupt end as the *Stella Vega* sailed towards Cape Wrath on the north-west tip of Scotland. Tommy had wondered why it was called Cape Wrath and now they were heading out towards the North Atlantic Ocean, he felt the difference immediately. The swell of the waves was much heavier and, as the bows plunged into each one, spray spread out from the forecastle making patterns like lace. Everything and everybody on deck was dripping wet and it felt cold.

The greasing was almost done and Tommy was feeling miserable when Danny spoke.

"Come on, Tommy, enough getting wet for now. You can help me in the hold."

The hold was a vast cavern in which voices bounded from the port side to the starboard side of the ship and back again. The Bosun was down there with some of the crew and they were sorting out nets and shackles, and preparing some wooden boards ready to divide the box-like pounds on deck when they started fishing.

Tommy could smell tar and oil, but the worst smell was the stench of the bits of rotting fish that had been trapped in the old nets. It made his stomach turn and he stuck his head into the neck of his guernsey. The waves pounding against the hull made everything shudder. The thought that only a slim sheet of metal separated him from the sea was scary, but Tommy felt a certain thrill. The movement of the *Stella Vega* was more noticeable down there. As the ship rose to the top of a wave, you rose with it. But it crashed down so quickly that it seemed your stomach was travelling at a much slower speed and stayed up in your throat. Again and again and again. So far this trip Tommy hadn't been sea-sick and he hoped he would not be, especially not now, down in the hold.

"Anybody seen Robert?" somebody shouted from the deck, trying to make himself heard above the noise of the pounding of the waves and the hiss and swish of the spray. Everybody in the hold looked from one to the other.

'Not again,' thought Tommy wishing, not for the first time that the Mate hadn't brought Robert on board.

Danny was rattled too. "Are we going to have to spend the whole trip looking for that lad?" he muttered.

Tommy joined a search party to go round the ship to look for Robert, and was teamed up with Danny. Together they checked the cabins, the washrooms and toilets, the galley and stores, while other people searched the engine room, the forecastle and the fish room in the hold. Meanwhile, the Mate was running around the *Stella Vega* shouting Robert's name. After what seemed like a very long time, Tommy and Danny went to the boat deck. There was no sign of the boy. But just as they turned to go back inside, Tommy saw something that didn't look quite right. The rope and the tarpaulin that covered the lifeboat looked as if it had been tampered with. He and Danny moved quickly over to the lifeboat and lifted the cover. Robert was fast asleep at the bottom of the boat. Danny ran off to tell everyone that Robert had been found.

CHAPTER SEVEN

Day two became day three, then day four, as the *Stella Vega* sailed due west through the long, lazy roll of the North Atlantic Ocean. Life on board had settled into a routine and it seemed that Robert had calmed down a little. It looked like the tellings off he got from the Skipper and other members of the crew had worked. He did disappear at times, but usually to his cabin or a corner of the mess where he would curl up, snuggled in his scarf, and read a comic or fall asleep. Even though he was not happy with the cabin he shared with Tommy, he returned there to sleep each night.

On their fourth night at sea, they were awoken by the rasping bark of the ship's fog-horn. Tommy jumped out of bed while Robert turned over and went back to sleep. The ship was no longer rolling over the waves, but moving ahead gently. All that could be heard was the powerful throb of the engines and the occasional blast of the fog-horn. Tommy made his way to the bridge where he found his father with the Mate, the Bosun and Norman, the Radio Operator. He looked out of the window and saw a dark grey cloud encircling and massaging the *Stella Vega*. The fog-horn sounded again.

"What is it, Dad?" he asked.

"Hello, son. Did we wake you? We often get fog banks

around here. Nothing we can do about it. Just keep our eyes and ears open." He laughed, "Did I say eyes? We'll be lucky. We can't see a blooming thing out there." And everybody else laughed, except Tommy. He didn't like the fog and the thought of not being able to see anything out in a vast open sea scared him. He went back to bed but couldn't sleep. He hoped they wouldn't crash into another ship or go aground in the thick fog. Then he remembered they had radar on board, and how easy it was to spot another ship, even in the fog. He hoped all the other ships had radar too.

Tommy had no idea what time it was when he woke up again. He saw Robert's bunk was empty so imagined it must be late. He'd be late for his chores and hated the thought of letting people down. He jumped out of bed to feel the ship rolling steadily, but he could no longer hear the fog-horn. He checked his watch and saw it was half past six. What a relief, it wasn't very late after all. He hurried to the mess where Brian was laying the tables.

"I'll give you a hand, Brian. The men will be here in a minute."

"I'm alright here Tommy, you go and help Cook."

It was warm in the galley and the smell of bacon and fresh bread wafted up his nostrils and right down to the back of his throat making his mouth water. Cook turned to him, saying,

"Grab yourself some breakfast before the vultures come in."

Tommy didn't hesitate for a second. He took three rashers of bacon, two fried eggs, a ladle full of beans, two 'doorstep' size slices of bread and butter and went into the mess where he scoffed the lot in record time. He hadn't realised how hungry he was. Just as he finished, the crew came scrambling in so he helped Brian serve their breakfasts. After breakfast, Tommy went to the bridge and asked, "Has the fog lifted?"

"Yes, hours ago. It was only a small bank and we'll come across plenty more on this trip. We're not far from Greenland now so Norman is checking the weather forecast and the radar screen. There could be some ice around here."

"Icebergs?" Tommy remembered the near miss they had had with an iceberg near Bear Island last year.

"Not only icebergs, ice floes and pack ice. A ship can get crushed if caught up in it."

Tommy didn't like the sound of that; he'd read about ships getting crushed by the ice when they were searching for the Northwest Passage but it hadn't occurred to him they'd be taking the same risks.

They sailed in the direction of Cape Farewell on the southern tip of Greenland, which he had heard some people call Cape Desolation or No Name Bank. He was surprised at how calm the sea was. He had expected the rough seas and storms they had encountered the previous year, but there was just the same long, lazy roll, where the waves didn't break over the slick undulating surface. They just rolled along, and the *Stella Vega* lolled from side to side as she steamed forward. Tommy spent some time in the Radio Room with Norman who was continually keeping a check on the weather forecast. The weather could change very quickly in these regions.

It was soon day five out at sea. The nets had been brought up on deck and secured and everything else they needed to start fishing was in place. Tommy was on the bridge during the afternoon when his father passed him a pair of binoculars and said,

"We should be getting near the coast of Greenland pretty soon. See if you can spot anything and let me know when you do."

Tommy lifted the binoculars and scoured the horizon. The sea was dark blue, nearly black in colour and shiny, and the sky was bright blue. Not a cloud to be seen anywhere. Not another ship in sight. He searched and searched and was beginning to get a bit bored until he spotted a ridge of clouds peeping up on the distant horizon. He kept his binoculars fixed on these clouds, and as they sailed closer he realised they were not clouds at all, but cliffs, great mountainous cliffs.

"Land, Dad!" he yelled, "I think I've spotted land."

The Skipper grabbed another pair of binoculars and trained them on the area Tommy was looking at.

"That's Greenland, son," he confirmed, "but it's still a long way off. We'll have had our tea before we get there."

Tommy skipped down to the galley to help get the tea ready feeling quite proud that he had been the first to spot Greenland. He told Brian and Cook, but all they could say was,

"Oh. Very nice," as they continued with their work. Tommy was disappointed they didn't share his excitement. He carried on with his chores in silence and after the meal Brian said to him,

"Don't be offended if we didn't sound overjoyed earlier. We've been to Greenland before, and it isn't the nicest place in the world. You'll see soon enough."

Tommy wondered what Brian was talking about. Bear Island wasn't a nice place either, but it was still an Arctic fishing ground. Why would it be different?

At about eight o'clock that night it was still daylight and Tommy was back on the bridge when Norman stuck his head out of the Radio Room, "Ice ahead, Skipper."

The Skipper picked up his binoculars and passed a spare pair to Tommy. Stretching out across the horizon they could see a faint white glimmer. It looked ghostly and cold.

"What's that, Dad?" Tommy asked in a voice that was almost a whisper.

"That's an Ice Blink. It's the light that hovers over the ice fields. We see it a long time before we see the ice itself." His father then checked their position and the radar screen.

Tommy kept is binoculars trained on the Ice Blink. He had never seen anything like it before and he didn't like it, but they were sailing right towards it. Some of the crew were out on the deck and they all stood in silence as they looked towards the light that stretched across the horizon in front of them. It was a long way off, but every man seemed to know what lay ahead and one by one, they returned to the warmth inside, heads held low and a gloomy, cheerless expression on their faces.

On moving closer to the light, Tommy spotted something in the water. It was a chunk of ice, not big enough to be an iceberg, but it was ice. He called his father and together they spotted another, then another.

"Pack ice. His father announced and, with Norman, they checked the radar to find a way round the approaching sea of ice. At that time of year field ice floated along the coastline stretching ten or fifteen miles out to sea. There were some loose bergy-bits, smaller chunks of ice that had broken off some of the icebergs. While the Skipper and the Radio Operator were checking the radar, the Bosun was at the wheel. He explained to Tommy,

"What we really have to look out for is growlers. Do you know what growlers are?"

Tommy shook his head and listened intently as the Bosun explained.

"Growlers are solid, very hard lumps of ice. They don't show up on the radar. They float just below the surface and you can only see a little bit of them when the weather is fine. They are a greenish colour. If there is a swell, they bounce up and down in the water. The swell can push them down into the water for quite a few feet, then, they shoot back up again really fast. Because they are made of such solid hard ice, if they shoot up and hit a ship they could easily punch a hole in the bow. We've got to keep our eyes open for growlers and we try to keep away from the ice fields, especially when it's dark and we can't see them."

Tommy's eyes opened wider and wider.

"We might have to force our way through the ice field for a while to get clear water. We need clear water for fishing."

Tommy stood in silence looking through the windows at the ice which was coming closer and closer to the ship, hundreds of small islands of ice. He began to understand why the crew had gloomy expressions on their faces when they saw the Ice Blink. The Skipper telegraphed the engine room to reduce speed. When they were surrounded Tommy could hear the ice grinding and scraping against the hull. Robert came flying onto the bridge shouting,

"What's that noise? What is it?" His face was ashen against the black and amber of his scarf and he was trembling.

"Come and stand here by me," Tommy tried to reassure him. "We can see everything from up here."

They were penetrating the icy gates of the Polar Sea as the bow of the *Stella Vega* sliced its way through. Tommy experienced a strange thrill of pleasure as he realised he was entering a new world, and all the tales of Arctic Adventure he had read about, flit before him vividly. He inhaled slowly through his nose and recognised the smell of the ice, the same stale, dank, mouldy old smell of the iceberg they had encountered near Bear Island. The Skipper and Norman studied the radar closely to find a safe passage through the ice. Tommy picked up the binoculars again and saw snow on top of the black rugged cliffs of Greenland which rose majestically, yet threateningly, high above the sea. Beyond, he saw the snow reached inland and mingled with the cold Arctic sky. The snow and the sky glowed pink in the low, evening sun. Further along the coast, Tommy saw the glistening surface of a glacier, streaked green, blue, white and black. As Tommy gazed at the Greenland coastline he realised there was no flat land. It was all mountains, harsh and rugged. They were very different from the mountains of Norway. For a start, there was no vegetation in this bleak looking place.

At last, the Skipper found the eastern edge of the ice pack and the *Stella Vega*'s prow was turned to the north as they entered the Davis Straight, keeping the land in view to the starboard side. Tommy jumped and his heart missed a beat as he heard a loud wailing sound. He looked to where the sound was coming from and saw Jeremiah Hobbs standing on the risen foredeck, holding on to the railings. He was able to distinguish the words,

"Joshua! Joshua! Are you there Joshua? It's me, Jeremiah. I've come to get you. I'm taking you home. Joshua!" These words were repeated again and again.

It was like being in a horror film and Tommy jumped when someone came up behind him. He was relieved when he saw it was his father.

Robert nodded towards the forecastle and asked, "What's the matter with him? Has he got a screw loose?"

Tommy turned to Robert, yet spoke softly, "No, he hasn't. Don't you worry about Mr Hobbs. My dad says he'll be alright when we start fishing." Then, looking at his father he asked,

"When are we going to start fishing?" He felt uneasy with the unearthly sound of Mr Hobbs echoing all around, mingling with the crushing and scraping of ice as the *Stella Vega* sliced its way through.

"All being well, first thing in the morning. We're going to sail up and down for a while to cut a path through the ice so that we have clear water for fishing. Why don't you and Robert go down for a game of draughts or dominoes?"

The two boys went to the mess where they found Brian and Cook playing draughts. They watched until the game had finished then the four of them settled down to a game of dominoes. Robert was enjoying the game and, it seemed, the company. Because of Robert's good mood there was a light-hearted, relaxed atmosphere in the mess. With all the worries and dangers they had to deal with outside, and the sound of the ice crunching and scraping against the side of the ship, not to mention a continuous spectral wailing, the last thing they needed was Robert's antics.

CHAPTER EIGHT

It was half past four in the morning when they heard,

"TRAWL DOWN!" as the Mate's voice echoed around the ship. It was time to fish and Tommy got up and hurried to the bridge.

Shooting a deep sea trawl was a dangerous and complicated manoeuvre even in the calmest sea and the warmest weather. It wasn't just the net going over the side, it was also bobbins, floats, cables, shackles and otter-boards. The whole lot weighed quite a few tons. It was lifted up and over the side of the ship attached to thick, strong wires which ran through the derrick. The timing of the manoeuvre had to be perfect. If the timing was wrong, then up to a dozen men on the deck were in danger of being swamped and crushed by the gear. The Mate was in charge of shooting the trawl and he was helped by the Bosun, or the Third Hand who was just below the Bosun in rank.

All the time they were shooting the trawl, Tommy heard the familiar sounds of metal banging and scraping against metal. He anticipated the strong smell of fish they were about to catch. He heard the loud voices of the men as they worked and the bellow of the Mate's or Bosun's voices as they gave their orders, their breath turning to steam in the chilled icy air of the early morning.

The cod end went into the water first, followed by the funnel part, or belly, of the net, then the bobbins and floats. At that point the otter-boards were clipped to the cables. The otter-boards were made of timber. They were longer than the tallest man and about as wide as his outstretched arms. They were very heavy and clipping them on and unclipping them off was a skilled and extremely dangerous job. The otter-boards kept the mouth of the net open wide while they were trawling the sea bed.

When the weather was icy, shooting the trawl was a problem. It was difficult for the men to hold their footing on the glassy deck. Their hands were half frozen, so their fingers weren't as flexible as they would normally be. The steel cables slipped on the icy barrels and men had to hang on to them to stop them from slipping out of position. It would be easy for a man to get his hands trapped.

While the net was being cast over the side, Tommy's father watched from the bridge windows, tense and alert. He occasionally leaned out of the window and barked an order to someone, and he and the Mate seemed to be having a silent conversation throughout the manoeuvre.

When all the gear was down, the ship steamed round in a circle until the trawl was astern. The Skipper then set a course and they steamed away, towing the net behind them. Now they were fishing. Tommy expected some of the men on deck to go inside for a break. But no, not straight away as jobs still had to be done. Wooden planks were lifted out of the hold and placed into position on the deck to make pounds, looking like square boxes fixed to the deck, ready for the fish to fall into when it was hauled.

"Where's my dad?" Robert appeared on the bridge.

Tommy beckoned him over to the window. "He's down on the deck. Look."

"Can I go and see him?"

The Skipper was prompt to reply, "Not just now. He's busy. You can wait up here if you like, until he comes in for a break. He won't be long."

"No thanks." A disappointed Robert turned and left the bridge.

Tommy and his father looked at each other and shrugged their shoulders, not knowing why Robert wouldn't want to wait for his father on the bridge. He would have been able to watch him and the men working on the deck. The Skipper asked, "Does he wear that scarf even when he's in bed?"

Tommy said nothing but smiled at his father who nodded back to him.

When he glanced at the clock, Tommy saw it was nearly time for breakfast.

"You'll be getting a few hungry men down there pretty soon," said his father with a wink.

Tommy expected to find Robert in the galley or in the mess, but he wasn't there so he got on with his chores of mashing tea and setting tables. He was deep in thought, remembering the stories he read about the brutal icy conditions during the search for the Northwest Passage. What had frightened him a lot were the tales of scurvy. He hadn't heard of it before reading those books and was horrified to find out what it was. It was caused by a lack of vitamin C, not eating enough fresh fruit and vegetables. It was a slow, painful death. With scurvy, the gums became soft and spongy and bled. The mouth and tongue turned black and the saliva turned black too. The skin, especially on the arms and legs turned purple and black and started to bleed. People who got scurvy also got acute, very smelly diarrhoea and they became more easily exposed to pneumonia and hypothermia. Tommy shuddered at the thought. At least he wouldn't be suffering the same hardships on this trip. There was plenty of fruit and vegetables in the store room. He wondered if he had lived all those years ago, would he have been brave enough to go on a voyage of exploration? A voyage into the unknown?

Loud voices coming from the passageway broke his thoughts. Robert was unceremoniously dragged into the mess by his father, the Mate. Robert was wearing his outdoor clothes and sea boots and was thrashing and struggling to break loose from his father, who roared,

"When the Skipper says you don't go outside it means you don't go outside. Do you hear me? I've just about had enough of your tricks young man and you can be sure this is the last time you come on board with me. I'm ashamed of you." The Mate was panting with rage.

"Get off me. I'll tell Mam you roughed me up. Anyway, I only wanted to see you working, that's all. I haven't done anything wrong," Robert whined.

"How many times do you have to be told it's dangerous when we're fishing? Men can die out there. And you can tell your Mam anything you like for all I care," the Mate continued, "It's about time she stopped spoiling you and treating you like a little lass."

"Well, why is it that Tommy's allowed out there sometimes?" Robert protested jealously.

"Tommy's got more sense in his little finger than you've got in the whole of your body. That's why." At those last words he stormed off.

"What are you looking at?" said Robert, glaring at Tommy. "Haven't you seen enough? It's all your fault anyway. You think you're clever, don't you? Just because you're the Skipper's son." Robert was sobbing with rage.

Tommy decided to say nothing as it might aggravate the situation, so he carried on setting the tables, turning his back on Robert who promptly stormed off.

"What was all that about?" Cook poked his head through the hatch.

"Nothing much," Tommy replied. "Robert not doing as he's told again."

Cook shook his head tutting to himself, and Tommy

worried what Robert might get up to next. He had seemed happy when they were playing dominoes, but you can't play dominoes all day, can you?

They fished all that day and Tommy did his usual chores of table setting, mashing the tea and helping Brian with the tayties. He spent some time on the bridge where he was allowed to take the wheel for short periods of time while they were towing, and he also went to see Norman in the Radio Room. The equipment in the Radio Room fascinated him. There were screens to look at, knobs to twiddle, the radio to communicate with other ships and, of course, the di-di-da-da of the morse code. Norman showed him a book of the morse code alphabet and told him he might want to learn to spell his name in morse. Tommy knew that the signal for SOS was dot dot dot dash dash dash dot dot dot, though he hoped he would never have to use it.

The only time they saw Robert was at meal times, but not to help with the chores. Robert didn't want to work and it was pointless trying to persuade him as he only threw a strop and marched off. The few times he went to the bridge he didn't stay long. One time, the Skipper allowed him to take the wheel for a spell, but had to stop him as Robert thought he was driving a racing car, making brum brum sounds and turning the wheel sharply to the left and to the right. Norman tried to get him interested in the Radio Room by explaining what each piece of equipment was and what it was used for, but Robert didn't want to know.

A group of deck hands went to the drying room to

collect their oilskin frocks before the start of one of their eighteen-hour shifts, only to find that someone had passed a length of string through all the sleeves, joining them all together. These hard-working men didn't have the time or the patience for practical jokes, especially silly playground jokes like that. They all pointed their finger at Robert, who, once again got a telling off.

CHAPTER NINE

Fish for breakfast, fish for dinner and fish for tea. That was all there was on the menu while they were fishing.

Tommy got up early the next morning leaving Robert fast asleep in his bunk. He hadn't slept well as Robert had tossed and turned for most of the night, keeping him awake. As he made his way to the galley he could smell the fish frying on the stove and his mouth watered in anticipation of devouring a huge cod sandwich for breakfast. He wouldn't have dreamt of having fried cod for breakfast at home, but at sea it was different. It felt special.

In the galley, Cook was showing Brian how to test when the fish was cooked to perfection.

"Anything I can do?" Tommy asked.

Brian turned to Tommy and flashing his crooked teeth said,

"Hiya Tommy. Guess who made the batter today?" and before Tommy had chance to reply, "Me! Cook showed me and I did all by myself."

Cook scoffed, "You don't have to be a scientist to learn how to make batter."

"I know," replied Brian, "but I want to be a cook one day

and who better to show me how to make batter than you. They say you're the best batter maker at sea."

"Flannel will get you nowhere, lad. Get on with your work." The Cook turned around and the boys smiled when they saw he was blushing.

"Shall I set the tables and mash the tea?" Tommy asked as he laughed at the banter between Cook and Brian.

"Yes and be quick. They'll be in any minute now." Cook was busying himself getting more fish ready for frying.

Tommy expected the mess to be empty, so he was startled by the figure of Jeremiah Hobbs sitting all alone in the corner as he entered the room. He took a step back in surprise, but said,

"Good morning Mr Hobbs."

Jeremiah Hobbs looked up at Tommy. His face was dark and weather hardened like tough old leather. His cheeks were red and blotchy with weather veins. His wrinkles were deep and pronounced and his eyes were tiny watery slits cut into his face. His hands, resting on the table, were like big shovels and his fingers reminded Tommy of thick sausages. Through his guernsey, Tommy could see that his forearms were wide and solid. Even though he was old, Jeremiah Hobbs looked a very strong man. Holding his head back to get a better look at Tommy, he drawled,

"Do I know you, boy?"

"My name's Tommy Ellis." Tommy stammered.

"Oh, the Skipper's boy." He nodded his head as he spoke. "I've heard all about you. Brave lad. Went overboard last year. The sea wasn't ready for you. It wasn't your time." He spoke with a deep vibrating monotone voice, very different to the wailing Tommy had heard the previous day.

"Don't be afraid, young man. I don't bite."

Tommy smiled at him and carried on with his chores.

Later that morning, Tommy was told to go out on deck to help Mr Hobbs.

The air was chilly but the weather was fine. The sky was clear of clouds, the ice was at a safe distance, and there was only a gentle swell over the sea. Sea birds screeched and swooped over the deck and all around the ship. Tommy felt lucky the weather had been so clement, even though it was bitterly cold and he had to wear his warm clothes. The deck hands were gutting the fish on the deck as quickly as they could, knowing that another bag full could be hauled in quite soon. The fish was cod. No sign of the halibut his father was hoping to catch. Tommy had only seen pictures of halibut and was eager to see a real one as they could grow to an enormous size.

As the sea was rather calm, he was able to sit on the foredeck with Jeremiah Hobbs mending nets. There was a lot of mending to do as the nets came up damaged with every haul. Greenland was well known for having a rugged, jagged sea bottom and a lot of the deck hands didn't like fishing there because of all the extra work mending nets. Mr

Hobbs didn't speak, but often looked up, his eyes scouring the horizon, as if searching for something, and Tommy didn't wish to disturb his thoughts.

Robert had also been allowed out on the deck and was giggling and screeching as he slithered and slid all over the place while following his father as he worked. One of the deck hands called him Merrylegs because of the difficulty he was having in keeping his legs steady on the slippery, rolling deck. Another deck hand shouted that they would put him in goal for Hull City next season as he might do a better job than the goalkeeper they had. The mood was jolly and the men's knives flashed as they gutted the fish.

The *Stella Vega* was fishing in the clear water of the Davis Straight between the ice sheet and the land. The ice sheet wasn't too far away and could be seen clearly, gleaming in the sunshine. It looked quite beautiful, but Tommy was aware of the threat the menacing ice held for them, and the mouldy smell was with them all the time. Whoever was on watch on the bridge kept a close eye on the ice, knowing that if it came close they would have to move quickly so as not to get stuck in its grasping jaws. Tommy looked up from the net he was mending and noticed something in the distance bobbing up and down between the waves. One minute it was there and the next minute it wasn't. He panicked, thinking it might have been a growler. He saw another, and another, and then another that was quite close to the *Stella Vega*. Tommy was shocked to see that it was a little boat with a man inside, and so far off shore. The little boat was full of cod and the man was standing up, legs apart to keep his balance. He was fishing with a hand line. He wasn't very well wrapped up, either. He wore nothing on his head and he had no gloves. He didn't even have an oilskin frock to protect him from the wind and the wet spray of the waves or the rain.

"He's a Dory man."

"What's that?"

Mr Hobbs put down his work and looked at the little boats round about.

"Somewhere around here is the mother ship. They put the boats out at dawn and the men fish all day and return to the ship at nightfall. But their work isn't done when they go back on board. They have to clean the fish and salt it before they go to bed. The next day they start all over again."

"Are they here all the time?"

"No, only during the summer months, but they stay here all summer. We think we've got a hard life, but those poor beggars have it much harder."

Tommy looked again at the man in the boat and at the others all around as they appeared then disappeared between the rise and fall of the waves. He looked up and saw a three-masted sailing ship in the distance, sails billowing in the wind as she gently ploughed her way through the gentle swell of the sea between the ice.

"Look at that!" Tommy said in awe.

"The mother ship. Portuguese." Hobbs spoke quietly yet

confidently.

"How do you know she's from Portugal?"

"Because only the Portuguese practice this type of fishing with sailing ships these days. They don't put the boats out when it's blowing a gale, but the weather can change quickly out at sea so sometimes they have to try to get back to the mother ship when it's blowing hard. However, they are more frightened of the fog. Bigger ships, like ours, can't see them on the radar and crash into them. Many have been lost that way.

Tommy grimaced. "That's awful."

"Yes, it is awful," Jeremiah Hobbs agreed before continuing, "and that's something else we've got to watch out for." Mr Hobbs nodded his head, looking straight ahead of them. Tommy focused his eyes on the direction the old man was indicating, only to see a small white dot in the distance. At least for now it looked like a small white dot, but Tommy knew it was an iceberg, and the *Stella Vega* was heading in that direction. Mr Hobbs had very good eyesight for his age and he didn't wear glasses.

"We'll be seeing a few more of those beasts while we're here."

"I saw them last year at Bear Island." Tommy shuddered as he recalled the night the Gallagher brothers were on watch on the bridge and they nearly hit an iceberg. "But we can see them on the radar, can't we?"

"Yes we can. Wonderful thing, radar. There was no radar on our Joshua's ship when she went down. No warning at all. But our Joshua was a good swimmer. I know he's out there somewhere, still alive and waiting for me to take him home." Then he shouted out loud through hands cupped around his mouth, "I know you're there Joshua. I'm coming to get you."

Everybody on deck stopped what they were doing and looked up to where Mr Hobbs was shouting again, and Tommy was sitting by his side feeling quite sorry for the old man, for he knew there was no chance of him finding his brother.

The silence on deck was broken by the Mate yelling at Robert once again, who was leaning over the side of the ship balancing on his elbows, swinging his legs from side to side.

"That boy shouldn't be here," Mr Hobbs groaned. "This is not a safe place for him."

Tommy agreed with Jeremiah Hobbs, but remained silent. He didn't want to admit he was afraid for Robert. With Mike's accident last year still fresh in his mind, he was well aware of the dangers that lurked everywhere on a trawler.

As the day passed and Tommy carried on working with Mr Hobbs mending the nets, the iceberg they had seen earlier grew closer, and more of them appeared as if out of nowhere. They looked beautiful as they glistened in the sunshine. Tommy was fascinated by one in particular. It looked like a cathedral with tall pointed spires, and in the centre there was an impressive archway, and you could see right through it. The colour if this iceberg was a luminous opalescent blue. It must have been about a mile away, but he could see how big it was as it towered dignified and noble above the rest. Looking around this Polar scene, Tommy was mesmerised. He felt calm and tranquil, yet his pulse was racing. How privileged he was to be a part of all this.

"You feel the call, don't you lad?" Jeremiah Hobbs was now closer to him and whispering.

"What call?"

"The call to the sea," Mr Hobbs continued in his deep monotone whisper. "Isn't everybody who feels the call."

Jeremiah Hobbs was scaring Tommy now and he wanted to get away from him. What was he talking about, 'the call to the sea'? What a load of old rubbish. He stood up and straightened his trousers. Then, the words hit him like a sharp flash:

'...*the call of the running tide,*

Is a wild call and a clear call that may not be denied.'

John Masefield's poem. Jeremiah Hobbs was right, he did feel the call. He turned to the old man and said,

"Well, it's been nice working with you Mr Hobbs, but I think it's time I went to see Cook to help out in the galley. See ya."

"You can come and have a yarn with me any time you want, lad," the older man said as he looked up at Tommy with deeper creases in the outside corners of his eyes and around his mouth.

'He's smiling at me,' Tommy thought as he climbed down to the main deck and hurried inside to the warmth of the galley.

CHAPTER TEN

Tommy's sleep was disturbed that night. He dreamt the icebergs had come alive and were calling to him. And once again, he was awoken in the early hours of the morning by the sound of the foghorn. He ran quickly along the passageways and up to the bridge. He was glad to see his father on watch so he said, panicking,

"Dad, if it's foggy, watch out for the Dory men."

His father smiled. "Don't worry lad, the Dory men don't fish at night. They're all safe and sound on their mother ship."

Tommy had forgotten Mr Hobbs had told him they returned to their ship at the end of the day.

"Go back to bed son. It's only half past two."

"I think I'll have a drink first. Do you want one, Dad?"

"I've got a tin of cocoa in my cabin," his father whispered to him. "Go and get it and make us both a cup of hot chocolate. Don't tell anyone else, mind. They'll all want one."

As they drank the hot chocolate, Tommy and his father talked about a film they had gone to see together at the Tower Cinema a couple of trips ago. It was a western called

'The Magnificent Seven' and it starred a very famous actor called Yul Brynner, who had a shiny bald head. They laughed when they remembered Tommy's mum was very cross with them when they got home, as each of them straddled an arm of the settee, pretending they were cowboys galloping on a horse. Since his last trip to sea, Tommy spent more time with his father when he was at home. He would also often go to the quayside to wait for the *Stella Vega* to come in at the end of a trip. As she came alongside, he would jump onto the deck and go up to the bridge to his father and stay there whilst they sailed through the lock and into the dock. No longer did he look upon his father as the stranger who came home for only a couple of days before going back to sea for another three weeks. When he was at home, his father now asked him about school, about how he was getting on in the school football team, and about his friends. The father and son sometimes had discussions about a programme they had seen on the television and Tommy's dad would explain if there was something Tommy hadn't understood. They had become firm friends. The mug of hot chocolate and the chit chat with his father seemed to soothe Tommy's nerves and he went straight to sleep when he got back into bed.

The fog had disappeared the next morning, but the icebergs were still all around. When Tommy arrived on the bridge after his morning chores in the mess and the galley, he saw they were about to haul in the gear, so he stood at the window and watched. He would never tire of watching these men at work and wished he was down on the deck working with them, as he had been on the last trip after

Mike's accident. The otter boards had been unclipped and the men were leaning over the starboard side, hauling in the net with each wave as it came closer to the ship. As the cod end came to the surface, there was a buzz of excitement as they knew this haul was special. Even the ever-present sea birds were screeching louder than they usually did. The crew worked together as quickly as they could to haul the net in. Once the cod end was lifted over the deck, everybody seemed to be holding their breath in anticipation as the Mate released the cod line at the bottom. The fish gushed out over the deck and there were loud cheers as halibut flapped and wriggled all around, wonderful Greenland halibut with their green coloured backs and their white bellies. One in particular was huge, well over six feet long. The men fixed a hook to its tail and hoisted it up. It was taller than any of the men down there. Tommy's father was leaning out of the bridge window hollering and cheering with the crew.

"We've done it! We've done it!" the Skipper yelled out again and again. "Hurry up and shoot the gear again. There's plenty more where that lot came from. Your pockets will be full at the end of this trip."

"Come down here, Tommy. I need your help." Cook was on the deck shouting up to the bridge window.

Tommy was worried he might have forgotten to do one of his jobs in the galley, or had he done something wrong? When he got to the deck he saw Cook was knee deep in halibut that were thrashing about around him. He picked one up, tossed it aside, then picked up another and another.

At last he came across a halibut which was nearly as tall as he was. He beckoned Tommy over and the two of them dragged the fish out of the pound.

"Don't let him go, Tommy. Hold tight or we'll lose him down the scuppers!" Cook was yelling, all excited and quivering. "By heck he's a fighter," he continued as the two of them battled with the enormous creature of the deep.

Everybody on the deck, and those on the bridge looking down at them, laughed and cheered as Tommy and the Cook wrestled and dragged the huge, thrashing fish out of the pounds and across the deck. It was a struggle as the fish didn't want to go with them and was fighting as though it was sensing its fate. It was slimy to touch and its fins were sharp, so they had to be careful not to cut or graze their hands or they would be very sore. They didn't want the halibut to go back into the sea again and were relieved when the Bosun came over and stunned the fish by bashing it over the head with a sledge-hammer. Both Tommy and the Cook lay stretched out on the deck beside the fish, their chests heaving, both of them out of breath. Tommy was panting as he croaked,

"It won't fit in the pan, Cook. It's too big."

The crew howled with laughter at Tommy's comment.

"Are you being a daft lad again?" Cook was panting too and his brow was glistening with sweat as he turned and smirked at Tommy. "I'm going to chop it up. It's halibut soup for tea tonight!"

The mood on board that day was light and cheery and even the Cook sang as he prepared the halibut soup. Tommy went back to the foredeck in the afternoon to help Mr Hobbs again, but there was no more talk of 'callings'. Robert kept getting into people's way and climbing about, but his father, the Mate, seemed to be keeping him under reasonable control. He was sent down into the fish room at one point to help store the fish on ice, but he didn't like that and soon came up again. After lunch he disappeared for a couple of hours, and the search party found him once again asleep in the lifeboat. He had been told not to go up there as he could easily have slipped on the railings he climbed up to get in the boat, but Robert being Robert, he didn't listen.

Tommy thought how lucky they had been to have such fine weather, even though it was bitterly cold. The sky was blue with hardly a cloud in sight. The sea was a deep shade of sapphire, dotted with white icebergs and in the distance was the carpet of ice which they kept an eye on at all times. With each breath Tommy felt the sharpness of the cold air. Not what he had expected at all after his experience at Bear Island. The storms on that trip were terrible and, at one stage they even caught the tail end of a hurricane.

Tommy spoke to Jeremiah Hobbs about what he had learned from reading books about the search for the Northwest Passage and the old man looked on showing interest as he spoke, without interrupting. The search for the Northwest Passage started not long after Columbus discovered San Salvador in 1492, thinking he had found a westward passage to India, hence the Caribbean islands being known as the West Indies. Over the centuries many expeditions had taken place, setting off from Europe, crossing the North Atlantic Ocean and heading north from Cape Farewell on the southern tip of Greenland, up the Davis Straight and through Baffin Bay to the islands north of Canada. All were hoping to find a quicker route to the nations in the far east of our planet. Each and every one of those expeditions had tales of freezing, icy conditions, frostbite, scurvy, misery, desperation, polar bears, hunger, death and, even cannibalism. Tommy spoke of Franklin's lost expedition.

"Captain Sir John Franklin was a Royal Navy Officer and an experienced explorer. He sailed from England in 1845 to search for the Northwest Passage which had never been navigated before. Including Franklin, there were one hundred and twenty eight men, but they were never seen again. Three years later in 1848, the Admiralty launched a search for the missing expedition and offered a reward. Many set sail in search of Franklin, but all they could find were the graves of three crewmen on Beechy Island and a few relics of the expedition. Searching the islands they found the remains of human bones, but there was no evidence of what had happened. Conditions were harsh and it seemed they had been overcome by the cold, the ice and, possibly hunger. It has been said that later, whaling ships coming to the area could sometimes hear the voices of the men of the lost expedition calling out over the ice." Tommy shivered as he ended the story.

Jeremiah Hobbs looked carefully at Tommy and said,

"My father was a whaling man, and his father before him. I remember sitting by the fire of an evening listening to the tales my father often told us. He told us of the ghosts of the ice, of the voices they heard calling out in the distance, especially when it was blowing a blizzard and the wind was coming from North West."

"But ghosts don't exist really, do they Mr Hobbs?"

"I don't know, Tommy lad. I don't know," he repeated before looking out over the dark icy sea as though he was searching for something in the distance.

Tommy followed the direction of the old man's gaze, but could only see the sea, the icebergs and the dark, looming cliffs of Greenland over the starboard bow. Was Jeremiah Hobbs seeing something else? Something invisible to Tommy?

"Hey boy! You boy!"

Tommy stood up, looked out over the whaleback and saw that one of the Dory men was calling to him and waving his arms. Tommy waved back and the man rowed closer. He steadied his boat and called again.

Tommy cupped his hands over his ears and leaning over the side towards the man shouted,

"What?"

The man repeated slowly, "Tomorrow – in – the – morning. I – come – get – you. You – fish – with – me, OK?"

Tommy was about to accept the invitation when Mr Hobbs said,

"You had better ask your father first, don't you think?"

Tommy signalled for the man to wait while he went to ask. His father came down to the deck with him and the Dory man asked,

"You Mr Skipper?"

"Yes, I'm Mr Skipper and this is my son," Tommy's father shouted.

"Oh I take good care of him. I promise. I good man."

The Skipper turned to his son and asked, "Do you want to go?"

"Yes please," said Tommy eagerly.

The Skipper turned to the Dory man and said, "OK. But only if the weather is good." To which the man replied.

"Is good. I know is good. I see you tomorrow, in the morning."

With a strange expression on his face, the Skipper shouted back to the man,

"Can you take two boys?"

The Dory man looked questioningly at the Skipper for a couple of seconds and said,

"Yes. OK. I take two." And with that he turned and

rowed his boat away.

Tommy turned to his father, feeling irritated that Robert would be going too. His father read his thoughts and said,

"At least we know he can't get into much mischief on that little boat. I'd better ask the Mate first, then we'll see if Robert wants to go."

Robert made such a fuss about not wanting to go on that rickety little wooden rowing boat. He said it would be cold and he'd get wet, so it was decided he'd spend the day in the galley with Cook, much to Cook and Brian's annoyance. Cook threatened to send him down to the fish room if he didn't behave, and Tommy was relieved he would be alone with the Portuguese fisherman.

CHAPTER ELEVEN

After a restless night, an excited Tommy was up early and checked the weather forecast for the day with Norman, who confirmed it would be fine. Cold, but fine. Cook had packed up some cold fried fish and two loaves of bread, as well as two flasks of tea to share. Tommy wore his rubber sea boots, oilskin frock and a woolly hat on his head. As a gift to the fisherman, he took a spare oilskin, another woolly hat and some cotton gloves. He was feeling a bit apprehensive at the thought of being in a small rowing boat, open to the elements, but he knew he would be safe with the *Stella Vega* close by. Tommy saw the little boat approaching as he looked through the bridge window.

"He's here, Dad. See you later," Tommy said as he left the bridge.

His father shouted after him,

"Enjoy yourself, son," and it seemed he was wishing he was going too.

Tommy climbed down a narrow rope ladder into the boat and his packed lunch and the gifts followed him. It was a difficult manoeuvre as the little boat was bobbing up and down next to the hull of the *Stella Vega* and he had to time it right before he jumped. Danny helped him over the side, telling him to be careful and not to let go of the ladder until he was in the boat. As his feet landed, Tommy looked up at the *Stella Vega* towering above him. A flash of fear ran through him, but soon passed as he knew he was not going too far away from the protection of 'his' mother ship. When they were safely away, Tommy noticed Jeremiah Hobbs on the raised foredeck, leaning on the railings. He didn't wave as he knew it was bad luck to wave someone off to sea, so he stared and nodded and Mr Hobbs nodded back in return. Did Tommy see a smile on Mr Hobbs's face? Immediately he noticed a different movement in the little boat compared to that of the *Stella Vega*. The *Stella Vega* rolled over the waves, but the little boat bobbed up and down with a jerking movement. It was going to take some getting used to and he was going to have to be very careful to keep his balance.

"What your name?" asked the fisherman, and pointing to himself continued, "Me Manoel. Manoel Tiago Rodriguez, from Viana do Castelo in Portugal." He spoke with a thick accent as the words rolled off his tongue.

Tommy pointed to himself, "My name's Tommy. Tommy Ellis from Hull in England. I'm pleased to meet you, Manoel."

"And I pleased to meet you Tommy Ellis. We now friends, yes?"

"Yes," Tommy agreed, "we now friends." And both of them laughed.

"How old you are?" Manoel asked.

"I'm thirteen. How old are you?"

"I older than you. I nineteen."

Nineteen? He looked much older than nineteen. That was probably due to being at sea in an open boat most of the time. Manoel wasn't very tall. He had deep wrinkles in the corners of his bright dark eyes, and his white teeth sparkled when he smiled or laughed. He was very happy with the gifts and donned the oilskin frock and woolly hat straightaway, posing as though for a photograph. Tommy clapped his hands and gave him the thumbs up sign, meaning he looked very nice.

"Where did you learn to speak English?" Tommy asked.

"In the school. Now Tommy Ellis, we work. I show you."

Tommy saw there were two coils of line in the bottom of the boat. Manoel picked up one with his left hand and raised it high above his head so that Tommy could see there was a large lead weight right at the end, then there were shorter lines coming from it at intervals and a large hook at the end of each. Manoel took hold of the first hook between the thumb and index finger on his left hand and with his right hand he picked up a piece of bait out of a big bucket and attached it carefully to the hook.

"Look, Tommy," Tommy liked the sound of Manoel's accent, "you must put the bait on strong so it will not come off in the sea. I do again." And he picked up the second hook, slowly repeating his actions so that Tommy could see. "Now you do it."

Tommy found the end of his line and carefully placed the large hook between his thumb and index finger, just as he had seen Manoel do. He then picked up a very slimy feeling, smelly piece of bait, wrinkling his nose with disgust as he did so, and fixed it on to the hook. He showed it to Manoel who checked it and said, "Bravo."

They both worked silently until all the hooks were baited, being careful not to get the line tangled up in the bottom of the boat. Manoel lifted the weight of his line over the side and, using both hands, eased the line down into the sea. There was a lot of line, which made Tommy wonder how deep the sea was. When Manoel had finished Tommy lifted his line over the side in the same way, his new friend watching all the time.

When the job was done they sat on a plank seat. There were two planks fixed to the boat so they had a seat each. Tommy was glad of his oilskin frock. Already it was glistening with the spray from the waves and it was protecting him from the cold breeze too.

"Where is other boy? Mr Skipper, he say two," Manoel asked.

"That's Robert. He didn't want to come so they are making him work in the galley today."

Manoel put his head to one side, squinted his eyes and asked,

"What eez galley?"

Tommy laughed. "It's the kitchen on a ship. Where we cook food." He mimed eating with a spoon as he spoke.

"Oh yes. I understand now. How you say? Galley?"

"Yes. That's right," Tommy confirmed.

"But why this boy no want come fish with you and me? He no like to fish? He miss beautiful day. Look," Manoel exclaimed, with his arms outstretched.

"He is missing a beautiful day. You are right Manoel," Tommy said with a big smile on his face looking around at the blue and white colours of the sea and the ice and the bright yellow of the sun.

While they waited to pull the line in, the two fishermen talked of their homes. Manoel said he had four brothers and two sisters. His brothers were fishermen like him and so was his father. But his father was dead. His father's boat did not come back to the mother ship one day. They searched all the next day but found nothing. He was gone. Manoel was only fourteen when that happened and as a result he had to leave school and start work. So he and his brothers fished to make money to take care of their mother and to help their sisters find husbands and get married. That was life in Portugal.

Tommy told Manoel he was sorry about the loss of his father. He told him that fishing on trawlers was dangerous too, especially in winter with all the ice and snow and the rough seas.

"You fisherman when you finish the school?" Manoel asked.

Tommy thought for a while before answering the question. "I want to go to sea, but I don't know if I want to be a fisherman. I haven't decided yet."

Manoel noticed the fishing lines were taut, so instructed Tommy to put on his gloves and copy him. Manoel did not wear his gloves. Slowly, using one hand after the other, they pulled on the line and as they pulled, they coiled it round in the bottom of the boat. It seemed to take ages. How far down had the lines gone? After what seemed a very long time, and the line becoming heavier and heavier, Tommy saw a silver flash beneath the water, and another below that. He pulled faster but Manoel said,

"Slowly Tommy, slowly. Like me. If you go too fast you lose the fish."

It was hard work and Tommy's arms and shoulders ached and burned as though they were on fire. He was wearing gloves, but his hands were chafing and sore inside them. How did Manoel manage without gloves? His skin must have been very tough. Tommy secretly hoped they didn't have a halibut at the end of the line, remembering the battle he and Cook had the previous day. They would never manage a halibut in that small rowing boat. He was relieved that the only fish they had caught was cod.

The cod they caught were well over a foot long, maybe even two feet long, like those caught by the *Stella Vega*, and they were lively, thrashing about as Tommy and Manoel tried to unhook them. They carried on thrashing when they were thrown into the bottom of the boat, one after the other. Tommy counted eighteen fish on that haul.

"Now we do again," Manoel sounded excited and once again they baited their lines and sank them down to the bottom of the sea.

Tommy took out the food Cook had given him and shared it with Manoel. All Manoel had to offer was dried beef which Tommy tried, but found it very hard to chew. After lunch they drank the hot tea from the flasks and carried on talking until it was time to haul again.

Throughout the day, Tommy kept an eye on the *Stella Vega*, hoping they didn't lose sight of her. Everything looked so much bigger from the tiny rowing boat, the waves, the icebergs, and even the cliffs of Greenland which appeared and disappeared as he and Manoel bobbed up and down between the waves. They baited the hooks and hauled in the fish another three times that day before Manoel said,

"Is late and we are full. I take you back now."

Tommy looked around and sure enough, the tiny boat was full nearly to the top with cod, and the sun was low in the sky on the western horizon. He felt sad having to go back, but at the same time he couldn't wait to see his father and tell him what a wonderful day he'd had. As they approached the *Stella Vega*, he saw Jeremiah Hobbs standing on the foredeck and wondered if he'd been there all day.

He recognised his father on the main deck with Danny, the Deckie Learner, waiting to help him on board. The rope ladder came down and before grabbing hold of it, Tommy turned to Manoel and said,

"Thank you Manoel. I've had a wonderful day today."

They looked into each other's eyes and both of them nodded as if to confirm the friendship that had formed between them. They didn't say 'goodbye' as they knew it was unlucky to say this word when going off to sea. Standing on the deck of the trawler, Tommy watched as Manoel rowed away, knowing he might never see him again. This young man had taught Tommy so much, not only how to fish with a hand line, how to appreciate the love and respect one has for the sea, but also how to appreciate the love and respect we have for our family and friends. As the little boat disappeared into the distance he said softly, "Stay safe Manoel Tiago Rodriguez. Stay safe my friend," not noticing the tears that were silently trickling down his cheeks.

That evening in the mess, Brian, the Galley Boy and even Danny, the Deckie Learner wanted to hear all about Tommy's day out on the Dory boat. They had seen them many times before when fishing around Greenland, but to actually spend a day in one was something else. Something very special. The only person not interested and trying to interrupt the conversation was Robert.

Brian turned to him and snarled,

"Will you shut up. We want to hear all about it."

"He's only showing off," Robert snapped.

"Listen clever clogs," Danny was annoyed, "you could have gone too. You just didn't want to. So there. Button it." He made a zipping-like motion across his mouth.

Robert stormed off in a huff and Tommy asked,

"What's he been doing all day?"

"Causing havoc, that's what he's been doing," Brian said. "He was supposed to be helping me and Cook. We gave him jobs to do, but he just ran off. They caught him up the radar scanner again, then they found him perched on the railings of the boat deck. In the end the Skipper sent him down to the fish room where the Bosun gave him some jobs to do. He wasn't happy though. Created such a fuss. He's nothing but a spoilt brat that one."

The three of them went out on the deck for a stroll before it got dark. It got dark very late in the far north during the summer months. They looked out to sea at the icebergs and compared them to shapes they were similar to back home. Brian pointed to one he said looked like the City Hall in Hull, and Danny saw one that he said looked like the New Holland Ferry, but soon spotted another, which he said looked like his sister's wedding cake.

Tommy pointed to the three-masted sailing ship in the distance,

"Look," he said to his companions. "The Portuguese mother ship. Manoel is on there."

The three young men looked over the sea to the sailing ship in silence, each in his own thoughts. Tommy was daydreaming about being on a sailing ship, but was interrupted by a movement over on the port side of the ship, together with a whooshing, blowing sound. He looked to where the noise was coming from and saw the tail of the whale lift out of the water and splash back down again.

"A whale! A whale! I've seen a whale. Look over there. It's coming up again." He pointed over the port side of the ship to where the whale leapt out of the water and thrashed back down into it. It was huge. Then there was another, and another. It looked like a whole school of whales. They were swimming together and the three boys watched in awe as the magnificent beasts played in the water, leaping up and thrashing down again. Tommy had seen films of whales back home, but he never imagined he would see on in real life. He loved it when the tail came up out of the water then crashed down again with a mighty smack. He could hear them breathing through the blow holes on top of their heads and saw water whoosh out, high into the air. They were entertained by the enormous whales for quite some time and were joined by other crew members who were not on watch. Everybody cheered as each whale leapt out of the water. One of them came up to the surface, rolled over and lay still alongside the *Stella Vega*. Tommy could see its eye and jaw open and it was looking up at them so he said,

"Hello whale." And he was hit by the fishy stink of the whale's breath.

In return the whale winked before disappearing under the water again. Everybody on deck had seen this amazing sight and Danny said softly,

"You've made another friend there, Tommy."

This was a day Tommy would remember for the rest of his life. Fishing all day in the Dory boat with his new friend, Manoel Tiago Rodriguez, and this evening, seeing real, live whales. Life couldn't be better than this.

Danny suddenly became serious. "I don't like the look of those clouds over there," he said, pointing forward in the direction the ship was sailing. "Let's go inside. I'm going to get some rest before the next watch."

CHAPTER TWELVE

Danny went to his cabin and Brian and Tommy went to the mess for a game of draughts. It wasn't long before the Mate poked his head through the mess doorway.

"There's a storm forecast so we're hauling now and lashing everything down ready to leave the area."

The crew members who were in the mess stood up immediately, went to get their oilskins and made their way out on deck. Greenland was a menacing place to be at any time, but in a storm it was very dangerous. Nowhere at sea was safe in a storm, but Greenland had field ice, icebergs and growlers. The quicker they got the gear on board and got away from there the better. Tommy thought of Manoel, but remembered Jeremiah Hobbs saying they didn't put the boats out when it was blowing a gale.

On the bridge, the Skipper was keeping an eye on the storm he could see approaching on the horizon.

"What happens now?" Tommy asked his father softly, afraid of disturbing his thoughts.

The Skipper checked the charts and said,

"I've decided the best thing for us will be to head for Goathaab, where there is a large bay for us to shelter from the storm. It will be rough, but not as bad as out at sea where there is the possibility of close encounters with icebergs, or even worse, to be hit by a growler.

Tommy looked out of the bridge window and watched as the men on the deck prepared for the net to be hauled. The winch motor chugged and whined as the cables and wires became taut, and strained to haul in the gear. The crew were ready to gut the fish and send it down to the fish room before securing the hatch. Both the Mate and the Bosun were shouting orders which each man obeyed without question. Tommy saw that the waves were no longer smooth and rolling, they had become choppy and the wind was blowing spray off the top of each crest as it rose out of the sea. The sky was no longer blue. It had turned a dark silvery grey colour, similar to the lead of a pencil, and the sea was also changing colour, from dark blue, to the frightening shade of dark green Tommy remembered from the storms at Bear Island. The movement of the *Stella Vega* had also changed to a bucking, jerking movement. Spray from the waves was now coming over the side onto the deck, and Tommy could see the white horses on the crests as they became higher and the wind became stronger. He could hear the wind whistling through the rigging of the ship, and the ropes and cables shuddered against the mast with a loud pinging noise. The sky grew darker by the minute and black clouds swirled angrily overhead.

Tommy looked on silently as his father checked the charts and Norman checked the radar and the depth of the sea around them and along the Greenland coast. Tommy felt he might be in the way so he said,

"I'll go down to the mess to make sure there's plenty of hot tea mashing for when the men come inside."

"Good idea, son. They'll need it. See you later," his father replied without even looking at him.

Tommy sensed his father was worried about the approaching storm, but he trusted him to lead them to safer waters. He had sometimes overheard comments from the crew about 'the old man', their way of referring to the Skipper. He heard things like, 'He knows what he's doing,' and 'He's a good Skipper.' Tommy was proud of his father, especially knowing he was respected by his crew.

The tea was mashing in the mess; cups, spoons, sugar and milk were ready nearby. Tommy sat alone at a table near the door, deep in thought as he listened to the changing rhythm of the engines as they strained against the ever-changing sea. He could also hear distant voices as the men worked, and wished he was out there with them. It was very hard work on the deck and last year he had been glad to help out as they were three men down after the Gallagher brothers left with the Russians and Mike had to be taken to hospital in Norway. It was as though he had stepped back in time to one year ago. The same shuddering of the ship as she strained to reach the top of a wave, then thump and tremor as she rode down into the trough before straining to reach the crest of the next wave. The same noises, clinking and clanging, metal grinding against metal and the whining of the winch motor as it struggled to haul in the net. The storm was getting worse. The tables were shaking and shuddering, the cups and plates in the galley were rattling and Tommy could also hear the swish and crash of the waves as they hit the deck above him. Cook and Brian were in the galley preparing the evening meal and there was nothing for Tommy to do until the men came in, except to sit there and wait, drumming his fingers on the table, following the sounds and movement of the *Stella Vega*.

Tommy's heart skipped a beat as he jolted upright, thinking, 'Robert!' Where was Robert? He shouted through to the galley,

"I'm going to look for Robert." And he was gone.

First he checked their cabin, then the washrooms and toilets, but Robert wasn't there. Tommy hoped the lad hadn't been stupid enough to go outside in the bad weather. He ran up and down the passageways checking store rooms and cabins, but no Robert. Tommy was beginning to panic. He went up to the bridge hoping to find the boy looking out of the window at the oncoming storm, but only his father and a deck hand were there. He looked in the Radio Room, but Robert wasn't there either.

"What are you looking for?" his father asked.

"Robert." Tommy's voice was deep and fearful.

The Skipper's face turned white. "Keep looking. Look everywhere you can think of. They've nearly finished on deck so I'll get a search party out. Tell Cook to hold back on the meal,"

The Cook slammed a large metal dish loudly into the sink when Tommy told him they couldn't find Robert. Brian asked,

"Can I help look for him, Cook?"

"Off you go," he replied before muttering under his breath, "I always said that boy was trouble."

A search party was organised on the deck to look for Robert. Robert's father was frantic with worry and fear that the boy had come to some harm. He ran from one end of the ship to the other shouting his son's name. The men looked inside the forecastle, down in the fish room, and some crew members even risked their own safety by climbing up to look inside the lifeboat, but they couldn't find Robert. After what seemed to be a very long time, the crew slowly and silently gathered in the mess. No one dared to speak, and everybody's head was hung low. The atmosphere was heavy and uncomfortable.

"Is the tea ready yet?" A little voice came from the doorway and everybody turned to see Robert standing there, hands in his pockets, legs splayed trying to keep his balance and the familiar Hull City scarf around his neck.

"Tell the Mate we've found him," someone shouted amid the hullabaloo of voices.

Robert couldn't understand why everybody was so upset and angry with him.

"I've only been in the engine room. It's warmer down

there."

One of the crew stepped forward as though he was going to grab hold of Robert, but another stopped him, saying,

"Leave it. He's not worth getting into trouble for." And the men ignored Robert as they sat down to have their meal.

Tommy went to him and said,

"Next time, tell somebody where you're going. Everybody's been looking all over the place for you."

Robert's father, the Mate, came storming into the mess. He grabbed hold of his son by the shoulders and, with eyes that were nearly popping out of his head, he glared at him with an expression on his face that was a mixture of relief and anger.

Tommy went to Brian and said,

"Maybe I should keep an eye on Robert, to see where he's going and what he's doing. He has no sense of danger at all."

Brian looked up and said,

"No, Tommy. You shouldn't be responsible for Robert. That's his father's job, not yours. Let's just hope that from now on the Mate doesn't let him out of his sight."

Tommy nodded his head in agreement, but he wasn't so sure. All he knew was that Robert couldn't be trusted and he was afraid for him. He didn't like Robert and wouldn't choose him as a friend, but remembering what happened to Mike the previous year, and him being older and more experienced, made Tommy feel uneasy.

CHAPTER THIRTEEN

The storm grew fierce during the night and Tommy didn't sleep well as he tossed and turned in his bunk. He kept waking up to the sound of the wind as it whipped around the ship, to the groaning and creaking sounds as ropes, cables and wires strained; to the echoing bang, bang, of a door which had not been secured. He looked over to where Robert was sleeping and heard his deep breathing, not quite a snore, but heavy just the same.

The *Stella Vega* was relatively safe in the shelter of the bay, just off the coast of Goathaab. There was nothing for the crew to do if they were not on watch, except play cards, dominoes or draughts, or to lie in their bunks and read some of the many magazines they had brought on board, or to catch up on their sleep.

Jeremiah Hobbs, however, preferred to be up on the bridge looking out of the window. Tommy found him there when he went to see his father after breakfast and said,

"Hello Mr Hobbs."

But there was no reply. Mr Hobbs was humming a tune that Tommy didn't recognise. He looked questioningly at his father who put his index finger over his lips and shook his head.

"Is it very bad out there, Dad?" Tommy whispered to his father, almost afraid of what the answer might be.

"Yes it is. Force nine to ten. That's pretty rough."

Tommy looked out of the window at the grey scene all around. Heavy rain was lashing the bridge windows, and on the deck below he could see the raindrops hit the surface then bounce off again in a frenetic rain dance. With each strong gust of wind the rain hit sideways on, skimming the deck. The wind screamed and screeched around the masts and through the rigging and the railings as it passed over the ship. The clouds were very low in the sky, low enough to reach out and touch. They were different shades of grey, ranging from a pearly, nearly white colour, to a dark, menacing nearly black shade of lead. All these colours gyrated round and round together, making Tommy think of the whirlpools he looked for when they sailed through the Pentland Firth. He didn't want to let his father know he was felling scared. The bow of the *Stella Vega* was pointing into the wind and some of the waves crashed over the whaleback and onto the deck, swishing and gurgling as they spilled out of the scuppers. The waves rushed past the ship towards the shore. Tommy looked out of the windows on the port side of the bridge. The tops of the cliffs on land were covered with clouds pushing their way inland. Waves raced from the open sea beyond the bay and hammered against the base of the cliffs, sending foam and spray upwards in an attempt to climb to the top. He noticed something in the distance.

"I can see some lights and buildings over there, Dad.

What is it?" Tommy asked as he pointed towards the coast.

"That's Goathaab. It's a small town. They have a small harbour and a few fishing boats. That's how they make their living," the Skipper replied, looking towards the coast.

Tommy went into the Radio Room and found Norman, with his earphones over his head, listening intently. His eyebrows were knitted together as he concentrated. He grabbed hold of a pen and wrote some figures on a pad which lay close by, at the same time scraping his chair backwards and throwing off his earphones.

"Skipper!" he shouted as he leapt through the door to the bridge. "Just got and S.O.S. from the *Cape Noli*. She's on fire, three miles due west of our present position." He passed the piece of paper with the coordinates of the other vessel to Tommy's father.

"They are right in the teeth of the storm." His face darkened before he continued, "We've got to assist. Any other vessels in the area?"

"No, Skipper. Only us."

Tommy's father reached out to a handle at the end of a pulley and pulled it giving six short blasts, then a long blast. The crew understood the signal meant emergency, all hands to the ready. There was trouble. Mr Hobbs said,

"I'll muster the crew in the mess for you, Skipper," and was gone before Tommy's father could thank him.

"Tommy." The Skipper turned to his son. "You and Robert are to stay in the mess until you are told to do otherwise. Do you understand me? I will call you both to the bridge when the time is right. Make sure Robert stays with you at all times. Do you get that?"

Tommy nodded his head, saying, "Yes, Dad. I understand." And was gone.

Tommy and Robert joined the crew in the mess and the Skipper told them all that another trawler, the *Cape Noli*, was on fire and in need of assistance. It was then Tommy found out it was an unwritten law at sea that if another ship was in trouble, you went to help them, in whatever way you could. No one spoke except to acknowledge the Skipper's instructions. "Aye aye Skipper," they repeated as they left the mess to prepare for the voyage into the unknown dangers that lay ahead.

For some of these men, this was not the first time they had been called to assist a trawler in difficulty. Tommy recalled one day, whilst they were sailing across the North Atlantic Ocean towards Greenland, Harry Hunter, the Bosun told him of the time in January 1955, he was on board one of the trawlers that went to assist the *Lorella* and the *Roderigo* during a freak storm off the north-west coast of Iceland. Both trawlers were top heavy with ice, both were taking water on board, and both foundered with all hands. He told Tommy that the trawlers going out to assist were also facing the same difficult conditions and were unable to reach the stricken vessels in time to help. Forty men from the city of

Hull were lost on that tragic day. Tommy shivered and got goose bumps as he remembered the story.

But this was August, and they didn't ice up in August, did they?

The Skipper returned to the bridge and took Tommy and Robert with him telling them they had to stay there until further notice.

The *Stella Vega* set sail to leave the safety of the bay heading due west, fighting furiously with the waves as they sailed into the wind. Tommy listened as his father and Norman stayed in contact with the *Cape Noli*. He heard that the fire was in the crew's quarters in the forecastle of the ship. The crew didn't sleep in the forecastle on the *Stella Vega*, which was quite a modern trawler, so Tommy assumed that the *Cape Noli* was an older vessel. He thought he wouldn't have liked to have to sleep in the forecastle of a ship, where the waves hit first. It must have been very noisy.

Tommy stood quietly on the bridge, holding on to a hand-rail to keep his balance, and continued to hear the conversation his father was having with the *Cape Noli*. He heard that there was only one casualty. One of the deck hands had burns to his face and forearms. Poor man.

Tommy looked at the time. It was twenty minutes to nine. It was as though the *Stella Vega* was being tossed inside a giant washing machine. Tommy could see nothing through the windows except the spray of the waves as they lashed the bridge. Jeremiah Hobbs was at the wheel.

"I'm bored, I want something to do," Robert whined as he held on to a hand-rail so as not to fall over due to the vigorous rocking of the ship.

"You're bored?" the Skipper shouted back at him. He picked a book off a shelf and thrust it into Robert's hands. Then, turning to Tommy, "Make sure he doesn't go out of that door. Sit on him if you have to."

Robert moved to the far corner of the bridge, sat on the floor with his back to the bridge casing, pulled his Hull City scarf up to cover his mouth and nose and opened the book.

Tommy was curious and said to him, "That looks good. What is it?" peering at the book Robert was holding in his hands, a dark blue hardback with silver writing down the spine that said, 'Trawlermen's Handbook.'

"We call that book, Handy Billy," said Tommy's father. "It comes in handy now and again."

Robert was obviously not in the mood to talk to anyone, so Tommy left him to read the book and went to stand by Jeremiah Hobbs at the wheel, holding on to the hand-rail so that he wasn't thrown to the floor as the *Stella Vega* fought her way through the storm. The engines whined as they strained and pushed her to the top of each wave where she teetered for a while before plunging down into the deep, dark valley before attacking the next wave. Over and over again, up and down, up and down, shuddering and jerking all the time, surrounded by the deafening howl of the wind and the hammering of the waves. Tommy could hear his father and Norman in the background as they communicated continually with the *Cape Noli*.

The *Stella Vega* was at the full mercy of the storm. The sky and the sea were as one. Black menacing clouds were shooting straight at them from the west, mingling with the savage waves all around, continuously attempting to seize hold of the ship with sharp watery talons.

"She should be coming into view any time now. We've got her clear on the radar," the Skipper shouted above the roar of the elements outside. As an afterthought he added, "I'm glad it isn't night time. We'd have an awful job finding her at night."

With butterflies in his stomach, Tommy raised the binoculars to scan the horizon. It wasn't easy with the mountainous waves coming at them from all directions, but he did spot what looked like a plume of black smoke in the distance.

"I think I can see her, Dad," he shouted.

His father came to stand by his side and picking up another pair of binoculars he trained them to where Tommy was pointing.

"Yes, that's her," the Skipper confirmed.

The atmosphere was tense on the bridge. Tommy turned towards Robert, thinking the lad might want to see the stricken trawler they were approaching, but he was still sitting in the same position, scarf around his nose and mouth, fully engrossed in the 'Trawlermen's Handbook', so Tommy decided to leave him there and say nothing. At least he wasn't causing any trouble.

As the *Stella Vega* struggled to sail closer to the *Cape Noli*, they saw there were two palls of smoke, one from the funnel, and one from the forecastle. However, by staying in contact with the Skipper and Radio Operator, they knew there were no more casualties. The Mate and the Bosun came to the bridge to await instructions from the Skipper.

They were where the storm was at its peak, three miles off the west coast of Greenland, out in the Davis Straight. Tommy wondered where the Portuguese sailing ship was and hoped they had found shelter from the storm. He thought of his day out fishing with Manoel. It seemed such a long time ago even though it was only a couple of days. He whispered under his breath, "Stay safe Manoel."

It was blowing a fierce gale and Tommy heard his father say force ten. The *Cape Noli* was very close, but they could not go alongside due to the heavy seas. It would be too dangerous as they could crash, risking the lives of both crews. The *Stella Vega* hovered at a safe distance from the stricken vessel, and it was decided between the two Skippers that the *Stella Vega* would sail side by side with the *Cape Noli* and escort her to Goathaab, about three miles away. Sailing back to the safety of Goathaab meant they would have the wind behind them, pushing all the way.

Tommy spoke to Jeremiah Hobbs, "At least with the wind pushing behind us, we'll get back there quicker than when we came out."

"Yes," Mr Hobbs replied, "If we don't get swamped by a wave, that is."

Rogue waves! So far this trip Tommy had not heard anyone shout 'Water!' when a giant wave was about to hit the ship. This was the first storm they had encountered. He froze as memories of being washed overboard on the last trip came flooding back to him. Feeling the icy cold water soaking through to his skin and filling his boots at the same time; being dragged down into the angry vortex trying to fight to stay afloat; gasping for breath to fill his aching lungs each time he came up to the surface; hearing a voice yell, "Swim Tommy, Swim"; learning that voice was his father who had dived in, risking his own life to save him. The recollection of it all brought a lump to his throat.

"But surely, Mr Hobbs," he said, trying to keep his voice steady, "The waves will lift us and carry us towards the shore, won't they?"

"We're not flippin' surfing out here," the old man snapped impatiently. "It doesn't work like that. Why do you think a ship has a high, pointed bit at the front? It's so we can cut into and through the waves. All we have aft is a short rounded end," Jeremiah Hobbs explained as he carried on steering the ship and Tommy felt stupid and embarrassed by his ignorance. Not once did Mr Hobbs let go of the wheel or turn to look at Tommy as he spoke. Tommy watched this experienced old fisherman, feet firmly planted on the deck, legs slightly apart and knees bent to steady himself against the movement of the ship.

Big waves did crash on the after deck and each time they did, it was as though the forward end of the *Stella Vega* was forcibly lifted up out of the water. Tommy didn't like it. In fact he was scared stiff, but didn't want to show his fear. His father came out of the Radio Room, leaving Norman to stay in touch with the *Cape Noli*.

"How's it going, Mr Hobbs?"

"We're steady, Skipper. She's a good ship."

"You're right, Mr Hobbs; she is a good ship." Then, turning to Tommy, "We're rocking and rolling again, aren't we son? Won't be long now before we're back in the bay where it's more sheltered. The fire on the *Cape Noli* has been put out and she is going to dock in Goathaab. The crew have done a grand job fighting the fire, but they have lost all their personal gear, their clothes and mattresses. They've wired the Company who told them to get new stuff and they'll pay for it."

Tommy knew that fishermen had to buy their own work clothes and even the mattresses they slept on.

"That's nice, but what about the man who got burnt?"

"They say there's a doctor in Goathaab who can look after him."

"Will he have to stay there like Mike had to stay in Norway?" Tommy had felt awful guilt at leaving Mike last year.

"Maybe not," his father reassured him. "He might be able to stay on board if they have plenty of burn cream and bandages for him. We'll see."

"But where will they sleep now their cabin has burnt?" Tommy asked.

"Probably in the mess. It won't be very comfortable, but it wasn't very comfortable in the forecastle either, especially in heavy seas with the waves coming at you and pounding the bows when you are trying to get some shut eye."

Tommy thought of the mess in the *Stella Vega* with the hard, wooden benches and he knew he wouldn't be very comfortable sleeping in there.

"Do they know how the fire started, Dad?"

"There's a stove in the forward sleeping quarters and a washing line hung across the cabin, over the stove, so the men can dry their socks and guernseys. Something must have slipped off the line in the rough sea and caught fire on the stove. As you know, a lot of the mattresses are made of straw, a donkey's breakfast they call them, and straw catches fire easily. When I was a Deckie Learner and then Deck Hand, I slept in the forward quarters on a straw mattress."

Tommy couldn't imagine his father being a Deckie Learner, but he must have been. All Skippers have worked their way up from the bottom and his father was no different to anybody else.

While they were chatting, Jeremiah Hobbs silently and expertly steered the ship as she was thrust forward, bows rising, then as the bow dropped with a loud thud, Tommy felt she was being dragged backwards before another wave pushed her forward again. All the time, Robert did not move from the floor of the bridge and he did not speak a word, except for the odd grunt when the ship came down hard onto the surface of the sea. He kept his nose in the book, now and again turning pages or turning the book on its side to study a diagram. He didn't show any sign of fear, or was he just indifferent to the danger they were in and to the fact that somebody was hurt?

CHAPTER FOURTEEN

The *Stella Vega* and the *Cape Noli* entered the bay side by side and both Skippers were relieved they had made it without further damage or injury to the crew. The *Stella Vega* dropped anchor in a secluded area of the bay while the *Cape Noli* continued to Goathaab, where she docked.

"I'm hungry."

Tommy, his father and Jeremiah Hobbs turned to look at Robert, still seated on the floor of the bridge with the 'Trawlermen's Handbook' in his hands.

The Skipper spoke to Tommy and Robert,

"Well, maybe it's time to go and help Cook. There'll be plenty of hungry men on this ship."

Robert was up and away without a word, leaving the book on the floor where he sat. Tommy picked it up, flicked through some of the pages and said,

"I'd like to read this one day."

"One day," his father replied solemnly and repeated, "One day." And took the book from his son.

...

It had taken a full day to go to the assistance of the *Cape*

Noli.

The storm had passed by the next morning and Tommy awoke to the welcoming sound of the ship's engines and the mouth-watering aroma of fresh bread. Robert was still asleep so Tommy crept out of the cabin on his tip-toes, carrying his boots in his hands, and made his way to the galley. The crew were already out on the deck so there was no one in the mess except Tommy and Brian. They both had fried cod sandwiches for breakfast, so big they had to be held in both hands, and two mugs each of steaming hot tea. Brian confessed to Tommy that he had been scared the previous day when they were out in the storm, especially when they were sailing back towards the bay. Tommy had been scared too, but being up on the bridge where he could see what was happening, and talking to his father, had seemed to soothe his nerves.

What a difference a day makes. The sky had changed from the low lying black, swirling, angry clouds, to a beautiful shade of bright blue. He thought of his mother who had a dress the same colour, and she called it sky blue. It was the first time he had thought of his mother since leaving home in the taxi with his father. The sun was a bright yellow ball and it reflected on the icebergs as they rose majestically out of the sea, shining opalescent white and blue, reflecting against the royal blue colour of the sea. Tommy wished he had his camera with him with a colour film. He'd been given a Kodak camera for Christmas. Next time he would bring his camera. The bright colours were deceiving though, as there was a slight breeze blowing off the sea which was bitterly cold and it slashed against Tommy's face. He stood on the foredeck, leaning lazily on the railings in awe of the sheer beauty of his surroundings. He saw the Portuguese mother ship sail out from behind an iceberg, sails billowing in the wind. He would love to go on a trip on a sailing ship one day. He searched for the Dory boats and saw a few, maybe five or six, quite some distance from the *Stella Vega*. Would Manoel be in one of the boats he could see? He would never know. Behind him, on the main deck, the crew were gutting fish, a mixture of cod and halibut, while they waited for the next haul.

Harry, the Bosun came up to join him and said, "Lovely, isn't it?" His false teeth carried on moving in his mouth for a second or two after he had finished speaking.

"Yes, it is," Tommy replied, turning round to look at the man, wondering if he was ever going to get a set of teeth that actually fit him.

"With a sea like this you should be able to spot the growlers easily enough."

Tommy had forgotten about the growlers and the thought of them lurking around just beneath the surface, like mines ready to explode, woke him from his trance.

"We've got some more nets to mend so come and give us a hand to drag them up, will you?" Harry's teeth clattered.

Tommy and Jeremiah Hobbs mended the nets on the foredeck all morning. Mr Hobbs asked him more questions about the books he had read on the search for the Northwest Passage, and in turn told him stories he had heard from his father about sailing up the Davis Straight to Baffin Bay when they hunted whales.

"The poor whales," Tommy commented. "They look so gentle."

"They are gentle," Mr Hobbs agreed. "But we used to get oil from them, to use in lamps and to make soap. Nothing was wasted though. The bones were used to make combs, cutlery handles and they were even used for women's corsets."

Tommy blushed and laughed. He remembered how he and his sisters giggled when one time they were visiting their grandmother, she had some pink corsets drying on the washing line.

It was when Tommy stood up to go to the galley to help with lunch that he realised he hadn't seen Robert all morning. The Mate, Robert's father, was on the deck, so where was Robert? When he got to the galley, Brian pulled him to one side and said,

"Just look at that. He's been sitting there with that book all morning."

"Would you believe it?" Tommy gasped, wide eyed at what he saw. "Looks like he's found something he's interested in after all. At least it's keeping him out of trouble, I'll see if he wants to help laying the tables."

Robert didn't want to help laying the tables. He picked

up his book and went off in a huff.

"He'll be back when he's hungry," Brian said.

After lunch, Tommy went to the bridge to see his Dad and told him how Robert had been in the mess all morning reading the book.

"Yes," his father replied. "He came up first thing and asked if he could borrow it. Looks like he might want to be a fisherman when he leaves school."

Tommy didn't reply to his father's last comment. He knew his father wasn't happy about him becoming a fisherman one day and thought it would be better to avoid the subject until he had made his decision.

The trawl was down and Tommy took the wheel for a while before going back to the foredeck to help Mr Hobbs mend the nets. He enjoyed steering the ship and he also enjoyed being out on the deck, especially with the weather being so fine, bitterly cold but fine. He enjoyed the chit chat he shared with his father, but he loved to hear the yarns from Jeremiah Hobbs about the olden days of fishing. Mr Hobbs sometimes spoke of his brother who was lost, and Tommy could see the pain of his loss was still etched on the old man's face. But Tommy knew that many families in Hull had lost at least one loved one whilst out fishing on the trawlers.

The sun was getting low in the sky over the western horizon and Tommy's hands and fingers were quite sore with the continuous handling of the nets. He put down the wooden needle he had been using and looked over the whaleback. The icebergs were still there, as beautiful as ever towering high above the waves, dominating the horizon, and there were some bergy bits, large chunks of ice that had broken away from the main icebergs. The ice floe was ever present towards the horizon. He saw some whales in the distance. They were leaping out of the sea in a graceful pirouette before thrashing back down again with their wide tail fins sticking upright in the air before disappearing into the depths of the Polar Sea. Although the whales were no longer a novelty to him he was still happy to stand and admire those wonderful beasts, happy to know they were not hunted any more, at least not by British ships.

One of the bergy bits, not too far away from the *Stella Vega*, looked as if it had something moving on the top. Tommy stood up and leant on the railings hoping to get a better view. At first he thought it was the wind blowing some loose ice along its surface, but he soon realised he was wrong. A polar bear stood up on all four legs and stretched its neck forwards, looking right at the *Stella Vega*. There was a small cub by its hind legs.

"Oh Mr Hobbs. Look at that!" he shouted, pointing in the direction of the bear.

"Oh dear. That's not a good sign. That bergy bit has drifted out to sea and it's too far for them to swim back to land. They could drown if they tried, especially the cub."

"Isn't there anything we can do to help them?" Tommy

pleaded.

"No, lad. Nothing we can do. We can't go up close to them as the mother will kill us straight away. They are very dangerous animals, especially when they have cubs."

The mother bear lifted her snout up towards the *Stella Vega* and growled, showing very long, very sharp, pointed teeth.

"But there must be something we can do, surely. We can't let them die." Tommy held on to the railings with both hands and shook his head. "I'm going to see my Dad. He might have an idea of how we can help them."

On his way to the bridge he wondered whether the close proximity of the bears would affect his asthma, but they weren't too close, were they?

The Skipper stood with his legs apart and his hands on his hips as he looked at Tommy saying, "How on earth can I help them? They are wild animals. Sometimes you've just got to let nature take its course, and things like this happen all the time. Anyway, you never know, they might get lucky if the wind changes direction and blows them back towards the land."

"But can't we tie a rope to the berg and tow it to the shore?" Tommy begged.

"You've got some wild ideas, son. No, we can't. I'm not risking my crew and we've already missed a day's fishing because of the storm. No. I'm sorry." The Skipper turned and entered the chart room at the back of the bridge.

Tommy knew that it was useless trying to convince his father. Once his mind was made up, that was it, he wouldn't change it. But there had to be a way. He left the bridge and stood on the deck looking at the mother bear and her cub.

"Sad, isn't it?" Brian had come to stand by Tommy's side.

"There must be something we can do," Tommy said, as if to himself.

"Come on. Cook wants us to give a hand with the meals." Brian turned away, leaving Tommy alone once more.

Tommy couldn't stop thinking about the polar bear and her cub, stuck on a lump of ice, far out to sea. When the evening meal was finished and everything had been cleaned and put away, he went to Robert who was sitting in the corner of the mess, still reading his book.

"There's a polar bear out there. Do you want to come and see?"

Robert lifted his face from the book, eyes flashing. "A polar bear? A real live polar bear?"

It was still daylight in the northern latitude, but the sun was low in the sky and the chilled air was biting in the breeze. Tommy was wearing his thick guernsey to keep him warm and Robert had put on his balaclava hat as well as the Hull City scarf he wore all the time. Robert's eyes came alive as he looked out towards the polar bears.

"Why don't we shoot them?" he asked, quivering with excitement.

Tommy was horrified. "We can't shoot them."

Robert danced on the deck chanting, "Shoot the bears. Shoot the bears. Shoot the bears." He pretended to be holding a rifle and took pot shots at the two creatures as they lay on their miniature island of ice.

"Bang. Bang. Bang," He shouted.

While he was dancing about, he didn't see the Bosun walking along the deck carrying a large bin and bumped into him with a thud. The Bosun, who hadn't seen Robert coming, dropped his bin and his false teeth shot out of his mouth and flew over the side of the ship and into the sea. The sight of Harry's teeth flying through the air made Tommy laugh out loud. When he saw that Harry was not amused he tried to stop laughing by holding his hands over his mouth to stifle the urge, but it was no use. Harry was furious and chased Robert around the deck. Tommy was joined by other crew members who had seen everything and they all laughed together with side-splitting belly laughs. They began to sing a famous cowboy song from a television series called 'Rawhide', about driving a herd of cattle across the wild west, and the words leapt out at Tommy.

Keep movin', movin', movin'.

Though they're disapprovin'

Keep those doggies movin'. Rawhide,

Don't try to understand 'em,

Just rope an' throw an' brand 'em
Soon we'll be livin' high and wide…

Throughout all the mayhem and raucous laughter on the deck, some of the words in the song kept repeating themselves inside Tommy's head, 'rope an' throw an' brand 'em…', 'rope an' throw an' brand 'em…' The idea came to him and he couldn't contain his excitement. They could throw a lasso around the berg and tow the bears closer to land. He ran to the bridge as quickly as he could.

"Dad! Dad!" he shouted. "I've got it. Listen. We could make a lasso and throw it over one of the pointed bits on the ice, then, we could drag it towards land. What do you say, Dad? Can we give it a try? Please?" Tommy begged his father.

The Skipper rubbed his hand over his prickly chin and looked pensive for a while before saying,

"You win. We'll give it a try." He opened the bridge window and yelled, "Does anybody know how to make a lasso?"

"What for?" One of the deck hands yelled back. "Are you going to tie young Merrylegs Robert to the mast?"

Once again there was a raucous laughter from the deck and Robert stopped in his tracks to look up at the Skipper who was still leaning out of the bridge window.

"Not this time," Tommy's father replied, laughing with the crew. "We're going to try to lasso that bergy bit and get the mother and cub closer to land."

Lengths of rope appeared as if out of nowhere, and all the men put their knot making skills into action to produce a lasso, each one of them trying to be the first to finish. It wasn't long before half a dozen deck-hands were standing at the port side of the ship swinging their lassoes round and round over their heads, up in the air before letting go to propel them towards the bergy bit and the bears.

There were shouts of encouragement, "Go on!", "Get in there!", "Yahoo!", as well as reassurance when they missed their target, "Nearly. Keep trying.", "Come on. You can do it!"

Robert was running from one deck-hand to the other, saying, "I want to have a go, let me have a go."

His father, the Mate, said, "Stand back Robert and let the men get on with it." But Robert ignored his father and carried on harassing the men.

Tommy watched the goings on from the foredeck and was laughing and chuckling at the antics just below him. Over on the ice, he saw the mother bear was eyeing them up suspiciously and he wanted to tell her not to worry, that they were only trying to help her.

"Got it!" everybody shouted together and Tommy saw that one of the ropes was secured around a high, pointed peak of the ice. The men, all holding onto the same piece of rope as though they were afraid to let go, moved steadily aft, to the boat deck, where their end of the rope was secured to the railings, just behind the lifeboat. The signal was given to the bridge that all was secure and the *Stella Vega* moved slowly towards the shore. The timing had been perfect as they had hauled the gear and were not going to shoot again until the next morning.

Tommy, Brian and Danny stood on the boat deck watching the confused looking mother bear and her cub that played around her feet. Cook arrived, struggling to carry a basket full of cod. Dropping the basket heavily onto the deck, he panted, "She'll be hungry, and so will the little one. See how far you can throw these."

The four of them each picked up a cod and hurled it towards the bergy bit, hoping it would land and not drop into the sea. Tommy's first attempt missed by a long way and Cook muttered, "Daft lad."

However, on the second attempt, Tommy's cod landed right at the bear's feet and he shouted, "Hurray!"

The bear sniffed it suspiciously at first, then, placing a giant paw on the tail, put her head down and her sharp teeth ripped the head off without any difficulty at all, before devouring the rest of the fish. One after the other, the fish landed at her feet and she lifted her nose towards the *Stella Vega* making a strange rumbling sound.

"She's saying, thank you," Tommy said.

Brian and Danny laughed, but Cook shook his head muttering,

"Talking bears. That's all we need. Lad's going daft again."

They heard a sound from behind them and turned to see Robert had climbed up onto the lifeboat cover. He was kneeling and pretended to hold a rifle in his hands, once again taking pot shots at the bears, "Bang. Bang. Bang."

No one spoke to Robert, as though they had mutually decided to ignore him. When the fish basket was empty, Cook picked it up and he and Danny left the deck. It was getting quite dark so Tommy and Brian decided to go inside too.

"Do you fancy a game of dominoes, Robert?" Tommy asked as they passed the lifeboat.

"Yeah, alright. I'm fed up with shooting bears," Robert jumped down to the deck and the three went inside.

Tommy was woken by Danny very early the next morning, at four o'clock.

"It's daylight and we're near the coast," he whispered. "We're going to let go of the bears."

Tommy slithered out of bed, already dressed from the night before. He pulled on his boots and quickly made his way to the boat deck. They were quite close to the shore, with cliffs of black, barren rock, covered with a mantel of thick, Arctic ice. There were deep, dark bays cut by the crevasses in the rock. Not far along the coast, to the north, was a glacier, and the early morning sun shone through it with a thousand shades of green, dark sapphire blue and amethyst. Tommy inhaled deeply and the familiar dank, musty smell of ice filled his nostrils. He looked out to sea and saw the horizon was shrouded in mist. He hoped it was only an early morning mist that would burn away as the sun rose in the sky.

"Let go," Harry, the Bosun, said. He looked very different without his teeth. His cheeks were sunken into his face and his chin was more prominent, as though trying to reach up and touch his nose. Tommy smiled as he remembered the Bosun's teeth flying out of his mouth the previous day, and how angry the man had been as he chased Robert around the deck.

The rope was released from the railings and the mother bear sensed that she was free. She looked towards the land before turning to stare at the *Stella Vega*, raising her nose in the air as a gesture of gratitude before diving into the water, followed by her cub. Tommy and all those present, watched in silence as the two animals swam towards the shore. He didn't know what the others were thinking, but he had a strange feeling of happiness and sadness at the same time. Happy the bears would have a chance to survive and sad to see them go. He turned to see his father, the Skipper, standing behind him.

"That's your good deed for the trip. Are you happy now, son?"

"Yes, Dad. Thank you," Tommy replied.

"Right you lot." The Skipper turned to the crew. "Let's go and get some more of that halibut."

CHAPTER FIFTEEN

The early morning mist had turned to thick fog by lunch time and it hung around for the rest of the day. The rasping croak of the fog-horn blasted out at regular intervals, and between each echoing blast, the silence was deafening. The fog they had encountered previously that trip swirled around the *Stella Vega*, but this fog remained still, shrouding the ship in a thick, choking blanket of grey wetness. Sparkling droplets of water hung from the railings, the cables and the wires. In fact, everything and everybody was dripping wet in this grey afternoon.

Some deck hands stood at the railings of the foredeck looking out as far as they could see, which was not very far, as the ship slid forwards at slow speed, slicing her way through the slick, black oily water below. Jeremiah Hobbs was also on the foredeck wailing and shouting for his brother.

"Joshua, I've come for you Joshua. It's me, Jeremiah. Give me a sign. Show me where you are." His voice drifted off into the distance, cutting through the dense fog. The unearthly sound made Tommy's skin crawl.

Other deck hands were in the pounds on the main deck, ignoring the lament from the foredeck, gutting the fish from the previous haul, getting ready to receive the next bag of cod from the net that was being dragged along the sea-bed as

124

they worked. Tommy sat alone inside the forecastle silently mending nets, worried sick they would hit a Dory man as he fished with his hand-line in the bitter cold, murky waters. Again he thought of his friend, Manoel Tiago Rodriguez, and inside his head he repeated again and again, "Stay safe Manoel. Stay safe Manoel."

Those who spoke on deck did so softly, as if afraid to awaken some unknown force that hovered around them. The only loud voice was that of Robert. He was acting the fool, pretending to be a ghost walking around the deck swinging stiff legs, holding gnarled hands and fingers out in front of him as he croaked, "I'm a ghost. I'm coming to get you."

The men did not like this as it made them feel uneasy, so the Mate, Robert's father, told him to stop fooling around or to go inside out of the way. Robert stood firm, and after adjusting his scarf around his neck and over his mouth, marched off with his hands in his pockets muttering under his breath,

"Umph. You can't even have a bit of a laugh here." Before he went inside.

Everybody on deck heard his words and some shook their heads in disapproval at the young lad's behaviour. Tommy was glad Robert didn't join him in the forecastle. Tommy wanted to get on with his work and be alone with his thoughts. He was well aware of the threat the fog held for them and, even though he was inside, the bark of the fog-horn reminded him of the danger. He couldn't stop shivering and he felt cold, a damp cold that seeped through his thick clothing and penetrated his bones. His fingers felt stiff as he worked with the wooden needle and the twine mending the gaping holes the jagged sea-bed had ripped through the net. He had already been told it was always the same at Greenland because of the sharp, rocky sea-bed and it meant extra work. The men would have a good pay packet at the end of the trip with the amount of fish, especially halibut, that was being caught, but they had more than earned every penny of it. This was harsh hunting ground. It was August and Tommy dreaded to imagine what it would be like in the winter. Once again his mind flashed back to the tales he had read about the brutal conditions the men had encountered during their search for the Northwest Passage.

"I'll take over while you go inside and get warm." Tommy was glad to hear Danny's voice waking him from his thoughts.

"Thanks Danny. I think my fingers have gone to sleep."

As Tommy stood up from his crouched position, his joints cracked and Danny laughed,

"You sound like a little old man. Go inside and get yourself a mug of hot tea. That will thaw you out."

"Thanks Danny. It's getting late and I should be helping Cook get the meal ready. See you later," Tommy said as he left the Deckie Learner to take over the mending.

The heat of the galley mixed with the smell of cooking hit Tommy full in the face when he stepped inside and his tummy rumbled.

"You look nithered, lad," he was greeted by a concerned sounding Cook, "but you'll have to mash your own tea. I told young Robert to do it, but he took himself off somewhere else, the lazy little monkey."

"Thanks Cook." Tommy didn't mind having to make his own tea. He asked, "Where's Brian?"

"Peeling tayties in the store room. Are you going to give him a hand?"

"Yes, and I'll take him a mug of tea," Tommy replied.

"As long as he drinks it while he's working. No time for tea breaks. I'll be needing those tayties soon. We can't keep the workers waiting for their fish and chips, can we now?" Cook replied sternly, but with a twinkle in his eye.

"Alright Cook," Tommy said. "With two of us peeling it won't take long."

Brian was glad of his mug of tea and as he worked, he saw that it took quite a few minutes for Tommy to start feeling warm again.

"You can see why I want to be a cook and I don't want to work on the deck. I'd much rather be warm and dry inside. The pay isn't as good, but it's better than the money I'd get if I worked ashore."

Tommy had heard from different people that the pay of the trawlermen was better than the pay of shore workers, but he didn't agree with Brian about wanting to work inside. Tommy liked to feel the fresh sea breeze and the salty spray on his face. He liked the feel of the ship rolling beneath him as he steadied his feet and bent his knees to keep his balance, riding the waves. He also liked to be up on the bridge where he could see everything that was happening on the deck and over the sea, especially when he was allowed to take the wheel and steer the ship. He liked to look out to the horizon where he could see changes in cloud formations and in the weather. Out there on the ocean, the sky and the sea were often as one, with no dividing line between. But sometimes, on a clear, sunny day, you could see the line by a distinct change of colour. Deep, dark blue for the sea, changing to a bright, paler blue for the sky.

"Are those tayties ready yet?" Cook bellowed along the passageway, making both Tommy and Brian jump.

"Coming Cook," Brian replied, and the two boys hurried to carry the bin of freshly peeled potatoes between them.

Some of the men slouched into the mess when the food was ready, most of them dragging their heels as they walked. They didn't have much time to eat before going outside again to relieve those who had stayed out on watch. They rubbed their hands together then cupped them and blew into them to warm up faster. Each man helped himself to the large fillets of battered cod ready and waiting on a huge platter, and the chips in a nearby, equally large bowl. The mess smelled like a fish and chip shop, especially when the salt and vinegar were sprinkled and splashed on every plate.

The men were subdued. There was not the usual loud banter of the fishermen in the mess. All that could be heard was the mutterings, moaning and groaning about the weather, while the fog-horn continued to croak its eerie background tune at regular intervals.

Tommy kept an eye on the teapot, which needed filling often as the men were drinking more than their usual share of tea. The first shift went back out onto the deck with their bellies full, the second shift came into the mess, and the scene was repeated. It was when the last of the dishes had been washed, dried and put away, that Tommy realised he hadn't seen Robert. It was strange as Robert was always among the first to eat at meal times.

He turned to Brian and said, "I haven't seen Robert, have you?"

"No, I haven't," Brian answered. "But he'll be asleep somewhere. There's plenty of fish left over if he wants to make himself a sandwich later on."

The fog did not lift, and later that evening, Tommy was on the bridge when he heard his father ask the Mate how much fish was in the hold.

"We'll get a good trip with what we've got," he said without telling the Skipper how much fish they had caught.

"That's it then." Tommy's father decided. "We're going home. Let's get out of this filthy place."

The Mate promptly left the bridge to tell the crew to

secure everything and put the gear away as the fishing was over for this trip.

CHAPTER SIXTEEN

Tommy was in the Radio Room with Norman who was intently looking at the radar screen to spot any obstacles that might be in their way. Brian appeared in the doorway, which Tommy thought strange as he hardly ever came to the bridge. He whispered to Tommy,

"Robert hasn't been for his tea yet."

"We'll go and look for him," Tommy whispered back, and the two boys left the bridge.

First they checked Robert and Tommy's cabin in case he had fallen asleep while reading a magazine as he had done a few times before. But no, he wasn't there. They went down into the engine room thinking Robert might have wanted to be in the warmest place on board. They spoke to the Chief Engineer who, with the second engineer and the greaser, searched everywhere, but Robert was not there either. What next? They checked the washrooms, toilets and went back to the mess in case he had shown up there, calling his name as they went. They couldn't find Robert. There were other places they could look, the lifeboat was a favourite place for Robert to hide, but they could also look in the fish room. Tommy had to tell his father. The deck was wet and slippery because of the fog and he didn't want to risk being out there without his father knowing.

A full search party was set up and Robert's father, the Mate, was frantic with worry and, at the same time, he was angry with his son.

"This is the first and last time he'll come to sea with me," he snarled to no one in particular, and carried on, "They said it would make a good lad out of him. They said it would do him good, make him more responsible for his actions. Well, it hasn't worked. I don't know what else to do with him. But he's not coming back to sea with me again. That's one thing for sure."

Inside, all the cabins, storerooms and cupboards were searched. They even searched the engine room again, but Robert was nowhere to be seen. Outside, the crew searched inside the forecastle, on the foredeck and in the fish room. Tommy and the Bosun went aft to look inside the lifeboat, but he wasn't there either. While they were on the boat deck looking around, Tommy spotted something out of the corner of his eye. There was looked like a piece of rag hanging over the railings. He went to it and took it in his hands. It was Robert's Hull City scarf. Clutching the scarf to his chest, Tommy turned to see a pair of eyes staring out of their sockets, towards him.

In a flash the Bosun was leaning over the railings shouting and yelling towards the water below,

"Robert! Robert!"

Other crew members came to the boat deck and one was heard to say urgently,

"I'm going to get the Skipper."

Nearly every member of the crew came to the boat deck and each one hung over the railings calling Robert's name. The air was filled with panic and fear.

Robert's father, the Mate, arrived and ran from one man to the other, yelling,

"What are you doing? Where's my son? Where's my Robert? He isn't out there. He doesn't like the cold. Come and help me look inside where it's warm, all of you, that's an order. Help me find my son. I know he's inside."

Trembling, Tommy came forward holding the black and amber scarf in his hands and held it out to Robert's father. The Mate stood still, the only movement his body made was the clenching and unclenching of his fists by his sides and the slow shaking of his head. The first sound he made was a faint murmur,

"No, no." The murmur soon changed to a heart wrenching scream, Nooo!" followed by, "He's inside. Help me look inside." He turned away and nearly knocked the Skipper off his feet as he stormed off the boat deck.

Tommy grabbed hold of the life-boat to steady himself and heard his father's fuzzy voice,

"Have you looked everywhere, Harry?"

"Everywhere, Skipper."

"When was the last time anybody saw him?" Turning to

Tommy he asked, "When was the last time you saw him?"

"It was this afternoon, Dad. I was in the forecastle mending nets and he was messing about on the deck.

"Did he go to the galley to help Cook?"

"No, Dad. He hasn't been doing his jobs for most of the trip. We didn't think anything of it. He only goes to the galley when he's hungry or if we're playing draughts or dominoes. We thought he'd fallen asleep somewhere and went to look for him. When we didn't find him we told you. That's all I know."

The Skipper looked desperate. "He could have gone overboard hours ago. I'll go and find his Dad. He's in a terrible state."

Tommy looked around at the men standing helplessly on the boat deck. Each face was gaunt and desolate. No one moved, no one dared speak. He looked up towards the sky and saw a star. The fog was lifting and a half moon hovered above, daring to show a glimmer of light that shone through the haze down onto the surface of the sea below. He looked out across the sea and in the dark, he could see the peaks of the icebergs peering over a low lying mist, faintly illuminated by the pale silvery blue glimmer of the moon.

Harry, the Bosun, came to stand by Tommy and whispered softly,

"The Skipper will probably get us to start searching the area at dawn. We won't be able to see anything in the dark, but we'll keep on shouting for him until it starts getting light. How many times was he told not to climb? If only he'd listened to us."

All Tommy could think of was the cold water, how cold he had been when he was swept overboard by a rogue wave the previous year on the trip to Bear Island. He remembered swirling round and round as he was dragged down into the depths of the icy sea, how he fought to breathe. The sea here was calm so maybe Robert was able to float to stay alive, maybe he's been able to swim and drag himself onto a small iceberg, But Tommy didn't know if Robert could swim. He told the Bosun what he was thinking in the hope that Robert would still be alive. But with tears in his eyes and a croak in his voice, the Bosun replied,

"The water is too cold to be able to survive more than about five minutes. In this temperature the body shuts down completely."

"Is there no hope at all?" Tommy pleaded.

"Very little." The Bosun put an arm on Tommy's shoulder and continued, "Why don't you go for a lie down? Get some rest before we start combing the area." He turned his head and called Danny over, telling him to go inside with Tommy. "Make sure he gets a hot drink down him, with lots of sugar."

Tommy tossed and turned in his bunk for the rest of the night. It was impossible to sleep with all the running about and people calling Robert's name. The Mate insisted that he was somewhere on board and that everybody should look for him. At first light, Tommy joined the men on the deck. The fog had cleared completely and a pale sun was rising in the east, above the cliffs of Greenland. He saw Jeremiah Hobbs on the forecastle with Danny and another couple of deck hands. All were leaning over the railings looking out over the water. Danny had a pair of binoculars held up with both hands as he searched and searched.

"Have a look at that bergy bit over there." Jeremiah Hobbs pointed towards a big lump of ice on the port side as he spoke to Danny, who immediately trained the binoculars in the direction Mr Hobbs was pointing, and focused on the position for a while.

"Nothing there," he said before scouring the sea once more.

The sea was a dark shade of blue with little white crests breaking on the surface as the rippling waves caught the breeze. The only sound that could be heard was the sluggish, pulsating vibration of the engines and the swish of the waves when they hit the bow as the *Stella Vega* made her way slowly through the water. There were no sea birds screeching and swooping across the sky, there were no clouds in the sky, but the air hung heavy all around them. There were no other ships to be seen, not even the Portuguese Dory boats. The Skipper had given orders to sail round and round in a wide circle so as to cover the area they had sailed through the previous day. Every man on board was searching.

Tommy's heart was heavy as he left the foredeck and made his way to the galley. He was hungry and he felt guilty for being hungry. Robert was lost and he was thinking about his stomach. It felt wrong, but he was hungry.

Before he reached the galley, the Mate came running to him and grabbed him by the shoulders,

"Where is he? Where's my Robert? Have you seen my Robert?" He shook Tommy's shoulders as he spoke.

Tommy could say nothing as he looked at the distraught, desperate face of the Mate. All he could do was shake his head.

"Steady on there, Jacko." Tommy's father spoke.

The Mate let go of Tommy who turned to stand by his father as he approached from behind him. Tommy's father put his arm around him and whispered hoarsely to the Mate,

"He's gone, Jacko. He's gone."

"He can't have gone." The Mate was shaking his head from side to side and crying, "I don't believe it. He's only ten. What will I tell his mother? She'll go mad. She'll never forgive me." He looked up and the pain he was suffering was clearly etched on his face.

The Mate pushed past Tommy and his father and rushed outside. They followed him as he ran to the boat deck. Men were standing around the railings searching the surrounding sea. The Mate saw Robert's Hull City scarf laid across the lifeboat. He walked slowly towards it, picked it up and buried his face in it as he sobbed, repeating his son's name,

Robert, Robert, Robert. Then he draped the scarf around his own neck and with an ear-piercing, blood-curdling scream, he ran to the railings grabbing the top with both hands, and leapt over the side howling,

"Robert!"

Tommy didn't understand why he was seeing all this in slow motion, and the voices he heard, "No! Jacko!" as everybody cried out together holding on to the railing where the Mate had jumped, were all muffled and distant.

One deck hand threw the lifebelt over the side hoping Jacko would grab hold of it and they could help him climb back on board. But he didn't move. He lay there in the water staring back at the *Stella Vega*.

"Take hold of the lifebelt. Swim to the lifebelt," everybody yelled, hoping to encourage him to try to save his own life, but Jacko didn't move. Tommy looked on in horror as the Mate's face slowly changed expression from desperation to quiet peace. Then a smile came upon his face before his body turned and he was face down, arms and legs spread apart as he slowly drifted away and eventually sank beneath the waves.

"Dad. Do something. You can't let him die," Tommy pleaded.

"It's too late son," his father wept. "He's gone."

Someone spotted Robert's Hull City scarf floating on the surface not far away and asked if they should try to pick it up.

"No," the Skipper replied. "Leave it where it is." He looked around at the distraught faces that surrounded him, each one looking to him, seeking solace and guidance, waiting for him to say something.

He cleared his throat before speaking in a voice that croaked with despair.

"In all the years I've been a Skipper," he stammered, "this has never happened on my ship. I am not a religious man, but maybe some of you are. I think we should gather all the crew here for a couple of minutes silence to show our respect. If anybody wants to pray, that's fine. Maybe you can say a prayer for those of us who don't know how to."

All the crew, with the Skipper and Tommy, stood together on the boat deck in one agonising, sobbing embrace, no one hiding their tears. After a while the Skipper lifted his head and spoke again,

"There's nothing more we can do here. Let's go home."

CHAPTER SEVENTEEN

It was not the first time a man had been lost at sea, and it wouldn't be the last. As the *Stella Vega* sailed across the North Atlantic Ocean heading towards the British Isles, the mood on board was solemn and subdued. Norman, the Radio Operator, contacted the Company back in Hull to tell them what had happened. Tommy was on the bridge one evening as they were passing Cape Wrath in the north west of Scotland. Since the Mate went overboard he couldn't stop thinking about when his own dad had jumped overboard last year, risking his life to save him. They could have both been lost, just like Robert and Jacko. There was a special bond between a father and his son, a feeling, deep within the soul that he could not describe. He was trembling and his heart was pounding inside his chest. He realised his father was watching him so he asked,

"What'll happen when we get home, Dad?"

"Everybody in Hull will know what's happened and there will most likely be a lot of people on the quayside waiting to see us in. It's always a sad affair when a fisherman is lost at sea, but Robert was only ten years old, and his dad to go too." The Skipper shook his head. "I can't imagine the state his mother will be in." After a few minutes silence he continued, "There'll be an inquest, of course. It might mean I have to take the next trip off to give evidence. We'll see.

I've already written a statement."

The expression on the Skipper's face mirrored Tommy's feelings; lost, cast away on a sea of pain.

...

The *Stella Vega* was passing the small seaside town of Withernsea, on approach to the Humber Estuary. Tommy was at the wheel and in his head he was going over and over the events of the trip, which, already seemed to have happened a million years ago, tarnished by the tragedy they had suffered. He remembered the whales; the icebergs; the polar bears; the Dory boats and his day fishing with his friend, Manoel Tiago Rodriguez; the storm and the fire on the *Cape Noli* and, of course the old man, Jeremiah Hobbs, calling for the brother lost many years before. He remembered how everyone had laughed when he helped the Cook drag the enormous halibut across the deck, and how the halibut soup was delicious. Would they catch halibut the next time he came fishing?

Next time? Would there be a next time? In his heart he knew there would always be a next time for going to sea.

They had caught plenty of fish this trip. The men would get a good pay packet when they got home. But at what price?

...

THE PRICE OF FISH

(Author unknown)

'The price of fish is very dear,

Two hundred men were lost last year.

Two hundred men in a watery grave,

That was the price, the price they paid.

Up in the land of the midnight sun,

Where the endless fight is never done.

Tired and weary, drenched and cold,

They strive to fill the iced-up hold.

And many a man's gone over the rail,

Lost in the teeth of an Arctic gale.

I only hope my point is clear,

The price of fish is VERY dear.'

Glossary of Terms

guernsey	thick, woollen sweater
Mate	second in command on the ship
Galley Boy	Cook's assistant
kit bag	funnel shaped bag used by seamen
Deckie Learner	young man learning the work on deck
balaclava hat	knitted hood-type hat
fearnought trousers	heavy duty work trousers
G.C.E	General Certificate in Education
Scuppers	holes at the side of ship's deck allowing water to flow out
ice floe	field of floating ice
pack ice	drifting ice packed together
bergy bits	large chunks of ice that have broken off an iceberg
Prow	the front part of a ship
flannel	to flatter someone
tayties	dialect word meaning 'potatoes'

48473210R00080

Made in the USA
Charleston, SC
05 November 2015